HANNAH WEST

in the Center of the Universe

A Mystery by
Linda Johns

DISCARDED

SLEUTH
PUFFIN

PUFFIN BOOKS

Published by the Penguin Group

Penguin Young Readers Group, 345 Hudson Street, New York, New York 10014, U.S.A.

Penguin Group (Canada), 10 Alcorn Avenue, Toronto, Ontario, Canada M4V 3B2
(a division of Pearson Penguin Canada Inc.)

Penguin Books Ltd, 80 Strand, London WC2R 0RL, England

Penguin Ireland, 25 St Stephen's Green, Dublin 2, Ireland (a division of Penguin Books Ltd)

Penguin Group (Australia), 250 Camberwell Road, Camberwell, Victoria 3124, Australia
(a division of Pearson Australia Group Pty Ltd)

Penguin Books India Pvt Ltd, 11 Community Centre, Panchsheel Park, New Delhi - 110 017, India

Penguin Group (NZ), Cnr Airborne and Rosedale Roads,
Albany, Auckland 1310, New Zealand (a division of Pearson New Zealand Ltd)

Penguin Books (South Africa) (Pty) Ltd, 24 Sturdee Avenue,
Rosebank, Johannesburg 2196, South Africa

Registered Offices: Penguin Books Ltd, 80 Strand, London WC2R 0RL, England

This Sleuth edition first published by Puffin Books,
a division of Penguin Young Readers Group, 2007

1 3 5 7 9 10 8 6 4 2

THE LIBRARY OF CONGRESS HAS CATALOGED THE PUFFIN SLEUTH EDITION AS FOLLOWS:

Johns, Linda.

Hannah West in the Center of the Universe / by Linda Johns.—Sleuth ed.

p. cm.

Summary: Hannah finds herself in the middle of a dognapping mystery while she and her
mother house-sit in Seattle's Fremont neighborhood, also known as the Center of the Universe.

ISBN-13: 978-0-14-240756-1

[1. Dogs—Fiction. 2. Housesitting—Fiction. 3. Seattle (Wash.)—Fiction.
4. Mystery and detective stories.] I. Title.

PZ7.J6219Hac 2007

[Fic]—dc22

2006026232

Puffin Sleuth ISBN: 978-0-14-240756-1

Printed in the United States of America

With thanks to my editor, Kristin

CHAPTER 1

"I HAVE A SURPRISE FOR YOU IN THE CAR," MOM SAID.

One could only hope it was a maple bar and a frosty blue Gatorade.

Practice was supposed to last just ninety minutes this morning, but we played more than two hours, and I was thirsty. I hadn't even noticed the time. That's just the way it is when I'm playing ultimate Frisbee. I'm still on the B team (you can probably guess that the A team is the best) for Cesar Chavez Middle School, but I'm getting a lot of play time this year.

Mom clicked the remote on her key chain to unlock the doors of our old Honda. The car chirped as it unlocked, simultaneously triggering something to pop up in the front passenger seat.

"Elvis!" I cried. I hurried to the car and opened the door, steadying myself as fifty-two pounds of hound came hurling toward me, covering me with slobbery kisses hello. "I'm so happy to see you!" I said, and I meant it. I find it's absolutely, positively impossible to be in a bad mood when there's a funny-looking basset hound around.

"Watch this," Mom said. "Elvis, backseat" she commanded. His long, wiggly body did a 180-degree turn and obediently went into the backseat, turning another 180 degrees until he was facing the front of the car. "Good boy. Now, sit," Mom instructed him. Elvis put his bottom on the backseat and leaned his front paws on the cup holder between the front seats.

"At least half of him is in the backseat," I said, buckling my seatbelt. "How come you already have the dog with you?"

"I dropped Piper off at the airport, and it seemed like it might be less stressful to Elvis if he didn't think he was being abandoned in the apartment. Piper says he gets a little woeful when she starts packing," Mom said.

I turned to look at the basset's droopy brown eyes and wrinkly face. "Doesn't he always look woeful?" I asked. As if responding to my rhetorical question, Elvis rested his chin on my shoulder and let out a sigh.

Elvis's owner, Piper Christensen, had hired Mom and me to stay in her apartment and take care of everything—including her dog—while she was in Hong Kong for an eight-week business trip.

You can look at Mom's and my life one of two ways: either we're homeless or we're professional house-sitters. I prefer to see our situation in professional house-sitting terms. The past year has been one house-sitting job after another, so we always had a roof over our heads. Lots of times, including this assignment, we've had some pretty nice roofs over our heads.

We headed down the hill from Bobby Morris Playfield, where I had just finished my marathon ultimate Frisbee session. Mom turned right on Sixth Avenue in downtown Seattle and headed north until we got to Lake Union and the Wooden Boat Center. I checked the street sign: Westlake. Out of habit I checked bus stops and bus numbers along the way: 16, 26, 28. It looked like those all headed toward our new home. We went past the group of houseboats where an old 1990s movie, *Sleepless in Seattle*, was filmed. I could see the Fremont Bridge ahead of us.

"There should be a law that more bridges are painted happy colors," I said, taking in the vivid orange and blue of the drawbridge that headed over the canal, connecting Queen Anne Hill and Seattle's Fremont neighborhood. As it turned out we had lots of time to enjoy the colors up close. Lights on the bridge started blinking, bells started ringing, and a metal barrier came down to stop cars from crossing the bridge. Mom turned off the engine, and we hopped out. Most people stay in their cars and wait, usually impatiently, for the bridge to lower so that traffic can start moving again. But unless it's pouring buckets of rain, Mom and I always get out to watch the action. This time a super-tall sailboat motored through.

"We'll probably be seeing this a lot," Mom said. "I heard that the bridge opens frequently."

"Approximately thirty-five times a day, making it one of the busiest drawbridges in the United States," I rattled off. In addition to checking out Metro bus schedules, I always research the history of whatever new neighborhood we are staying in—however temporary it might be.

The bridge deck lowered, car engines started, and traffic began moving both ways across the bridge.

When our car reached the other side, Mom turned to me with a grand gesture and said, "Welcome to the Center of the Universe."

"Huh?"

CHAPTER 2

"I THOUGHT YOU RESEARCHED ALL OF THIS," MOM SAID.

"D'oh!" I said. How could I forget? The Fremont neighborhood had dubbed itself the Center of the Universe. According to my research on Wikipedia, residents of this area of Seattle, about three miles north of downtown, referred to their neighborhood either as the People's Republic of Fremont or as the Center of the Universe. I wasn't exactly sure why, except that Fremont had gone from a hippie haven to a high-priced neighborhood with trendy restaurants.

"Darn it, I'm in the wrong lane to turn. I'm going to have to go around the block," Mom said. The extra drive was okay with me. I liked looking at the restaurants and shops, and this way we'd get to go right by one of Seattle's most famous statues.

"Go slow here! I want to see what the people are wearing today," I said to Mom. We were right next to this cast-aluminum sculpture of six life-sized figures—including a little dog—huddled together as if they were waiting for a bus or a train or something. It's officially called *Waiting for the Interurban*, so I guess they're supposed to be waiting for the train. They don't exactly look happy, but I guess I wouldn't be either if I'd been waiting a few decades for a train that never comes. The thing I like best is that people put costumes on the bus people statues. According to Wikipedia, this is usually done in the middle of the night so that in the morning they have fresh outfits, hats, balloons, signs, and even umbrellas if there's a chance of rain and scarves around their necks when it's cold. Kind of like dressing a permanent snowman.

Today must have been Western theme day. The metal people wore cowboy hats and bandannas. A large sign said, "Happy Birthday, Trixie!" The little dog had a blue bandanna tied around his neck and a party hat on his head. Someone had taped a yellow sign to the dog's tail. The traffic light turned green and we started moving, so I couldn't read what the yellow sign said.

We soon came to a very tall building, and I realized I was looking at the Epi. That's the name of the apartment building where we were going to live. It's actually called the Epicenter, as in the Center of the Center of the Universe, but Piper told us people just call it "the Epi." Purple and blue served as a backdrop for metal swirls on the outside of the six-story building. It was whimsical and fun, proving that not all adults take themselves too seriously. I loved it. Seriously loved it.

"How totally cool is this?" I asked as Mom turned into the alley and into the parking garage below a big supermarket. "I'm so excited to live above a grocery store. Snickers bars just an elevator ride away."

"I wouldn't count on that," Mom said, laughing. Elvis added a bark. "I'll take him, so you can take these two." She handed me my goldfish, Vincent and Pollock. They were inside a Ziploc bag that I'd placed inside their glass bowl so the water wouldn't slosh out.

Mom and I have this ritual about moving into a new place: we always save our most precious belongings for the final load. Luckily for me, Mom and her friend Nina had moved most of our stuff to Piper's apartment earlier in the day while I was at ultimate Frisbee. I really had only one trip to make upstairs to carry my current sketchbook, backup sketchbooks (one can never have too many), and some photos in my messenger bag. I picked up a painting I did at art camp and the bowl with my fish.

We'd be able to go straight from underground

parking garage to fourth-floor apartment via elevator. But the elevator stopped on the lobby floor.

"Hold the elevator, please," a man called. He was pinning a bright yellow flyer to the bulletin board in the lobby. I could see the word "Missing" in big letters. It looked like the same sign I'd seen taped to the dog statue.

"Thanks," he said as he got on the elevator. Elvis tried to sniff his pockets. "Sorry, but I don't have anything for you, Elvis," he said.

"So you know Elvis?" Mom said. "We'll be taking care of him and Piper's apartment for the next two months. My name is Maggie West, and this is my daughter, Hannah West."

He looked at both of us. He didn't look happy. Not mad. Just sort of sad. Maybe preoccupied.

I moved my fingers in an attempt to wave without dropping my goldfish.

The man nodded. I noticed he wasn't offering up his name or any details. He took a roll of tape from his coat pocket and started taping the corner of a yellow flyer to the elevator wall. The stack of papers he'd been carrying scattered on the floor just as we got to the fourth floor and the elevator doors opened.

"Let me help you," I said. Mom pushed the button

to keep the elevator door open while I put down my belongings and knelt to pick up papers.

"Oh, no! Is it your dog that's lost?" I said, finally getting a good look at the yellow flyer that said "Missing."

"He's not lost. He's missing. Boris disappeared earlier today," he said dejectedly, handing a flyer to me as we headed into the hallway.

A blurry photo of a dog was centered at the top of the page. Below its picture it said:

Missing!
Please help find Boris, a two-year-old bichon frise. Disappeared Saturday morning. Last seen on the sidewalk outside Joe's Special. Reward!!!

"Do you think he was stolen? Snatched? Maybe even dognapped?" I asked. Mom gave me that stern parent look that usually means, in my case, "Stop jumping to conclusions."

"That's exactly what I think," the man said. "One second he was there. The next he was gone. Vanished. Vamoosed. I'm Ted, by the way. I live three doors down from Piper. She made sure everyone on this floor knew that you two were coming to house-sit and take care of Elvis."

"We appreciate that," Mom said. "Let us know what we can do to help find your dog." I knew Mom was sincere, but it sounded like one of those things people automatically say when they don't think they can possibly help.

"I can definitely help track him down," I said.

I fished a business card out of my pocket and handed it to Ted.

HANNAH J. WEST
PET SITTER, DOG WALKER, PLANT WATERER
AND ALL-AROUND ERRAND GIRL
235-6628

Ted gave me a slight smile, but I don't think he took my offer seriously. He had other things on his mind.

But I already had an idea about what I could do to help.

CHAPTER 3

"I HAVE TO CALL LILY," I SAID, PRACTICALLY MOWING MOM OVER IN THE entryway to apartment 409 and running down the hall to the kitchen. I'd been to Piper's apartment twice before to meet Elvis, so I knew exactly where to go. I needed to get to a water source and my cell phone. When you move around as much as we do, you cling to whatever rituals and traditions you have. One of mine was to call Lily within seconds of moving to our new pad. The other one was to get Vincent and Pollock into their bowl as soon as possible. Mom disappeared farther down the hallway to the living room to call her friend Nina.

In a total show of ambidexterity, I used my left hand to dial Lily's phone number and my right hand to pour Vincent and Pollock into their bowl.

"Lily! It's me. I'm at the new apartment, and I think I may have already found my next case," I said, wiping

11

up the water I'd spilled all over the kitchen counter. Apparently I'd overestimated my ambidextrous abilities.

"A new case? I haven't dried off from our last one," she said. "Does this one include television appearances?"

"Um, excuse me. Who needs TV when we've got real-life action?" Here we were, typical middle schoolers by day and cunning detectives by night, yet Lily was more interested in whether we could talk our way into being extras on a TV show like we were over the summer, on the set of *Dockside Blues*.

"Well, you don't exactly make money in the crime-solving business," she said.

She had a point. We had each made a hundred bucks as extras in that cable TV drama. But our brush with fame also put us in the middle of a mystery. Which we'd solved, of course.

"This case has a significant reward," I said, trying to entice her.

"Okay, you've got my attention now," she said.

"A dog is missing from our new apartment building," I said. "There are signs all over the neighborhood about it."

Silence on the other end of the phone. Then, a big sigh. "Hannah, a missing dog is hardly a crime. Granted, it's heartbreaking, but the pooch could be seeking kibble elsewhere. A lost dog does not indicate criminal activity."

Now it was my turn to sigh. Lily, of all people, should know to trust my intuition on these things. "It might not officially be a dognapping—yet. I still want to do some digging around. Did I mention there's a reward?"

"I'm sure I can convince my dad to give me a ride over there. He's all excited about you and Maggie living on top of one of the Puget Sound Co-op Natural Markets, better known in our house as PCC," she said.

"Great," I said. "I'll see you soon." I tried to hide the disappointment in my voice. It's not that I wasn't excited to see Lily—I was. After all, she was my best friend. It was the fact that her dad was excited about PCC Natural Market that was bumming me out. I've learned from experience that the kinds of markets that get Dan Shannon excited are not the kinds of super-markets that carry Snickers bars.

While I waited for Lily to arrive, I looked around for the best place to put Vincent and Pollock's fishbowl so it would be safe from the dog. Elvis might have short legs, but Piper had warned us that his long body makes it so he can "counter surf," rise up on his back legs and reach the kitchen counters. He does it in search of food, but I didn't want to take any chances.

"Whoa!" I said, carrying the fishbowl into the living room. When I'd visited the apartment before it had been nighttime. I could tell there was a view, but I had no idea that the corner windows would have such a spectacular view of the canal. Those metal swirls that decorated the outside of the building actually over-lapped part of the windows, almost as if punctuating the view. I put my fish on top of a small hutch and headed back down the hall. I pushed the two doors that were ajar all the way open, and was thrilled to see that they were both bedrooms. One was obviously Piper's—my mom would use that one. So I checked out the other one.

"Whoa!" I said again. No one had told me I was going to have my own bathroom and a walk-in closet. I bopped across the hall to check out Mom's bedroom, which also had a bathroom and walk-in closet. "My" bedroom, however, had two added bonuses: a TV and a velvet-covered chaise longue for my TV-watching comfort. "This place seems almost as big as our old house," I said a bit wistfully. I missed having a real home that we could call our own.

"Actually it's a bit bigger than our old house. About two hundred square feet bigger," Mom said.

I unpacked my clothes and hung them in the walk-in

closet. They took up about one-hundredth of the closet space. I arranged my books, sketchbooks, CDs, and photos on the bookshelves. I guess the good thing about having sold most of our possessions is that unpacking takes only about nine minutes.

I was checking out the television channels at my disposal (at least ninety) when Lily buzzed. "Quick, let me up!" she said frantically over the intercom. "My dad is threatening to drag me into the grocery store and give me a tour of the produce aisle and tell me which vegetables are the highest source of vitamin K or Q or whatever."

I buzzed her in and told her how to get to our new apartment. I know it's not really "our" apartment, but it's too clunky to say "the apartment where we're house-sitting" or even "Piper's apartment."

When she got up to the aparment, I gave Lily the grand tour, leading her down the hallway and showing off the bedrooms and the bright kitchen. I saved the view for last. "Whoa," Lily exclaimed, echoing my earlier amazement. I had to admit, it was an impressive view.

We headed back into "my" bedroom, and I showed Lily the bright yellow flyer.

"Look! See how there are three exclamation points after the word reward?" I asked.

"The overuse of exclamation points, in addition to being irritating, is usually done by those who are trying to make something out of nothing," Lily said. "In this case, I bet it means a teensy tiny reward for a teensy tiny dog."

I pulled out my copy of *Legacy of the Dog*, a book about dog breeds that I've practically memorized. I quickly turned to the toy group section and found a two-page spread on the bichon frise. "Meet the *bee-shahn free-zay*, so much more than what you call a teensy-tiny *chien*," I said, trying to sound French to pique Lily's interest. But I knew once Lily saw photos of this little white fluffy dog she'd be hooked, with or without my lame attempt at an accent.

"Oh, look," she practically cooed. "Its name means 'curly-haired puppy.' We have to help find this little fluff ball." We read about the bichon frise together, learning that it was only about ten inches tall, weighed only about ten pounds, and has been around since the Middle Ages. The book also noted that the breed has a "pretentious gait," which I think could also be interpreted as the dog has a happy, jaunty walk. My preschool teacher at Montessori Garden had a dog like this named Bijoux, and it was about the sweetest dog I've ever met.

"It sounds like the perfect dog. Ack!" Lily squealed as she looked down. "And speaking of dogs, you must be Elvis."

Piper's basset hound was licking Lily's wrist, an act of sincere friendliness that Lily seemed unable to fully appreciate.

"Come here, Elvis," I said, and immediately the hound transferred his licking to me. "Look at these ears! How could you not love these velvety soft ears?" I asked, petting Elvis's eight-inch-long brown ears.

"And look at all this extra skin," Lily said, grabbing hunks of skin around his neck. "He looks like old, fat Elvis Presley from the 1970s, not young, cute Elvis from the 1950s. Eww! He stinks, too."

"He doesn't stink. He just has a distinctive houndy odor. He also has a magnificent nose, second only to a bloodhound in terms of its power. And, I might add, he's of French descent."

"Uh-huh. He still stinks," Lily said.

I have to admit Elvis did smell kind of doggy. It's a good thing basset hounds are so cute. Their long bodies, short legs, sad faces, and soulful eyes make them pretty irresistible. I could tell he was winning Lily's devotion. She started singing "You ain't nothing but a hound dog" in a twisted attempt to sound like Elvis Presley.

"Maybe Elvis will be my new sidekick. He can track Boris. You know, Columbo had a basset," I said. I love old 1970s and 1980s detective TV shows, and one of my favorites is *Columbo*, where this seemingly absent-minded detective in a trench coat brilliantly solved cases in an understated way.

"I hate to tell you that you're not Columbo. You're not even Sherlock Holmes. And Elvis is no hound of the Baskervilles," Lily said. We recently read *The Hound of the Baskervilles* in Language Arts. The horrific hound causing centuries of havoc in that story was nothing like the sweet basset hound lying next to me.

I know that I'm no Sherlock. But I believed that there was something going on behind Boris's disappearance.

I have a nose for these things.

Elvis rubbed his cold nose against my arm, as if he agreed.

CHAPTER 4

ELVIS NUDGED MY ARM HARDER, AND I REALIZED THAT HE MAY NOT HAVE been agreeing with me as much as he was trying to tell me he needed to go outside.

"Perfect!" Mom said, as I walked into the living room to get Elvis's leash. "Lily, Hannah, get your coats. We'll check out the neighborhood together, with Elvis as a tour guide."

Elvis was ready to lead us, practically pulling us out of the building, through the alley, and up a short flight of stairs that led to Fremont Avenue. Mom was the real tour guide, though, making sure that I knew cross streets and landmarks. Let me tell you, Fremont has some great landmarks. We were walking down Thirty-fifth, and all of a sudden there was this fifty-foot silver rocket on the corner. Across the street was Norm's, a restaurant that lets you bring dogs inside. We peeked inside just to make sure it really would be okay to come back with our dog.

"Well-behaved dogs are always welcome here, as long as the humans are well behaved, too," a man behind the bar said.

As we left Norm's, someone called out, "Elvis has left the building." Apparently everyone really does know Elvis around here.

We kept going, looking at the sights. Besides the bus people statue, there's a tall bronze statue of Vladimir Lenin on a patio outside of a Mexican restaurant. I don't even really know who Lenin was, but according to the sign next to the statue he had been a communist leader of the Soviet Union.

We walked along slowly, allowing Elvis to sniff at whatever he liked while we checked out the windows of a couple of clothing stores and Fremont Place Books. We peeked in at Frank and Dunya, a store that sold pieces by local artists and that had sculpted dogs—named Frank and Dunya, the owner's former dogs—ready to greet us. Mom wasn't kidding when she said that people in Fremont really loved their dogs.

Close to the canal was Costas Opa, a Greek restaurant we go to at least once a year when my mom's cousin is in town. We walked along the canal a little bit, and then we went into Capers, the housewares and home-furnishings store where Mom's friend Polly Summers works. She's the one who set up this house-sitting and dog-sitting gig for us.

"Believe me, you'll need some of this," Polly said, showing us these candles and fragrance sprays called Fresh Wave. "Piper buys this stuff all the time to cover up those houndy smells. No offense, Elvis."

Finally we came to the spot I wanted to visit. Joe's Special. "Hey," I said. "This is the place where Boris was snatched." I started to look around, to see if I could spot any evidence.

"We don't know that the dog was snatched, Hannah," Mom said, with just a bit of warning in her voice.

Ted's yellow "missing" flyers were posted on both windows of the restaurant. Elvis started sniffing around. "Look! He's sniffing for clues! Maybe he's going to track Boris," I said.

"Or maybe he found a piece of bread," Lily added, as Elvis hoovered up a snack and followed his taste treat with a fit of barking. A *long* fit of barking.

"Shhh!" I tried.

"Quiet!" Mom said.

"Hush!" Lily said.

"Try 'quiet, please,'" said another voice. Elvis stopped barking. Immediately. The first thing I saw was a huge

21

sheepdoglike dog, but at the end of the dog's leash was a guy, maybe around our age. But you can never really tell with boys. In my seventh-grade homeroom, there was a twelve-inch difference between these two guys, Garth and Caleb, who are best friends and have birthdays in the same month.

"I guess that worked," Mom said. "Is that some kind of universal dog command that we don't know?" Mom asked.

"Nah. I just know that Piper uses the phrase 'quiet, please' in that tone of voice, kind of soft and nice, if you know what I mean. It's the only thing that gets Elvis to stop barking sometimes. If you yell or say something loud, he'll just bark more to try to be heard. Kind of like he's in a contest to outbark you." He looked as if he was sizing us up.

"We're Elvis's dog-sitters, taking care of him for Piper," I said. I didn't want some stranger thinking that we were dognapping Elvis.

"Cool. Piper said to be on the lookout for you guys. This is Scooter. He and Elvis are good pals," the shaggy-dog guy said. The two dogs were sniffing each other happily.

"It's nice to know that people know each other's dogs and are watching out for them," Mom said. "Especially since one of our neighbors just lost his dog."

"I saw the flyer. It doesn't sound like Boris is lost,"

Shaggy-Dog Guy said. He looked at his watch. "I gotta go. Nice meeting you."

Only we didn't really meet him.

"He never said his name," Lily pointed out. "Then again, we didn't tell him ours either."

"Yeah, but he did say that he thinks Boris was dognapped," I said.

"Hannah!" Lily and Mom said together, which got Elvis barking again.

"Quiet, please," I said nicely to Elvis. It worked. "Okay, he didn't actually say dognapped, but he implied that he thought something was up, too." Elvis was pulling his leash over to a bowl of water labeled "Fresh Dog Water." The window above was painted with the store's name, "The Perfect Pet: Grooming, Treats, Toys."

"Hey, I know that woman," I said, pointing to the woman at the counter inside. "She volunteers at the animal shelter." I waved. She looked right at us but didn't wave back. Maybe the sun was in her eyes or something.

"Um, Maggie, I need to go, too. My dad is picking me up soon. We have to go to this symphony thing tonight. My parents have decided we need some culture in our lives," Lily said.

We headed back to our building. Yellow flyers with Boris's photo were in every shop window. Every window except The Perfect Pet, that is.

CHAPTER 5

"HERE YOU GO, IZZIE," I SAID, PLACING A FRESH BOWL OF WATER IN FRONT of my new best friend the next morning. Mom had dropped me off at the Elliott Bay Animal Shelter on Sunday morning for my weekly volunteer job. "Actually, you're one of my three best friends," I said, scratching behind her ears. "I just worry the most about you."

A beam of sunlight came through the window and lit up a triangle of Izzie's gleaming brown fur. I interpreted this as a sign that things were going to get better for this love muffin of a dog. Izzie looked at me and hesitated, as if making sure it was okay to go to the bowl.

"Go ahead, it's for you," I said. She slurped the water eagerly. An enthusiastic head shaking after her drink sprayed water everywhere. She turned back to me and rested her chin against my thigh. My heart ached to think what kind of a life Izzie must have had. I have a pretty good imagination, but I just couldn't understand how someone could mistreat an animal. "Especially you, Izzie," I said, scratching her behind her right ear. The ray of sunlight was now hitting the exact outline of a white patch of fur on her nose. I decided to take that as an even bigger sign that things were about to get better for this dog.

Izzie and I have a lot in common. We're both technically homeless (I already told you about that), we're both smart (if I do say so myself), and I'm adopted and she's going to be adopted. I used all my positive-thinking energy about her getting adopted, and soon.

Izzie had come to the Elliott Bay Dog Shelter last month. She brought along the equivalent of an entire city of fleas. The poor thing was an itchy, scratchy, miserable mess. Big chunks of fur were missing because she had hot spots, which is what happens when a dog has fleas and is supersensitive to them. I was there the day she arrived. We didn't know much about her at first, except that she was itchy, sensitive (to fleas and in spirit), and timid. By the second week a little more of her personality was showing through, and it was time to photograph her and get an ad up on the Web site to find her a new home.

I asked Leonard if I could take a stab at writing her ad. Here's what I wrote:

> Leggy, svelte, smart, sensitive, and sweet adult female looking for the perfect match. Loves long walks in the woods, taking scenic rides in your car with the windows rolled down, listening to all kinds of music, eating quiet dinners in the kitchen, snuggling on the couch, and relaxing by a fire.

Leonard made me take out the "leggy" part because he said it was starting to sound too much like the ads grown-ups use to try to find true love on those Web sites that have words like *harmony* and *love* in their names. That, of course, was the whole point. I'd read in the newspaper about an animal shelter that placed a funny ad like that and got hundreds of calls for a Labrador puppy named Daisy. Of course, I'd also read that the Daisy story was an urban legend. Anyway, if there's one thing I learned in the Cesar Chavez Middle School Writing Workshop, it's that first drafts need to be rewritten. Here's my revision:

> Meet Izzie, a smart, sensitive, and sweet adult female dog, approximately five years old. This large mixed-breed (Lab, maybe some rottweiler, and dogs from other diverse backgrounds) has good manners and is eager to please. Knows basic commands and is

a fast learner, especially if there's a tasty treat as a reward. Gets along well with the other dogs and cats at the shelter and is gentle with children. Needs regular exercise but is calm and quiet. She has a mysterious past and came to us with fleas, but she's in good health now. Spayed, up-to-date vaccines, and ready for you.

"Nice job, Hannah," Leonard said, even though he still made some edits to the ad. "Working on another sketch of Izzie?"

"She's a good model for me," I said, showing Leonard the latest of the dozen drawings I have of Izzie. I closed my sketchpad and put it back in my messenger bag. "May I take Izzie for another short walk and then help with her bath?"

"Sure. I'll let Meredith know you're bringing Izzie in for a bath and a nail trim. And Hannah," Leonard said, "I know how hard it is to say good-bye to animals, but you have to keep in mind that our job is to find them homes where they'll be safe and loved for the rest of their lives."

I smiled at him, but I still felt like my moist eyes were giving away the fact that I was pretty close to tears. I had been coming to the Elliott Bay Animal Shelter every week for the past couple of months, giving me more than five times as many hours I needed for my community-service requirement at school. Not that community service should even be a requirement. I felt like I should be paying the shelter for the opportunity to be here. In fact, I decided to set aside half of the money I make from dog-walking for the rest of the year and donate it to the shelter.

Fifteen minutes later Izzie and I were back at the shelter and waiting for bath time. A volunteer in the grooming room was finishing up with a huge dog the size of a real-life Scooby-Doo. When she turned around, I realized it was the volunteer who I saw at The Perfect Pet yesterday—Meredith.

"Meredith? Are you ready for us?" I asked tentatively.

"Just finishing up with Cyrano, here," she said. She towel-dried him and clasped a wide collar around his massive neck. I brought a ramp over to the table so that Cyrano could walk down from the grooming table.

"Cyrano is about to go home with a new family," Meredith said. She sighed a long, deep sound that sounded so sad.

"It must be really hard to say good-bye to dogs, even when you know they're going to good homes," I said, paraphrasing what Leonard had just said to me.

"It's not just that," Meredith said, all doom and gloom. "I'd say only five percent of the people who have dogs are worthy of them."

I laughed nervously. She was kidding, right? Oops. I guess not, because she glared at me. I pretended to cough.

"I guess I'm not sure what you mean," I said.

"I don't have any exact figures. No one's ever bothered doing a scientific study on something as important as responsible dog ownership. But I see way too many dogs in my job who are neglected," she said.

"Do you mean your job at The Perfect Pet? I think I saw you there," I said.

She glared at me.

"Did you? Hmmm. Why don't you bring Izzie up here," she said. I noticed she used a soft, sweet voice to talk to dogs. Her voice to me wasn't nearly as sweet.

Izzie pranced easily up the ramp, but then she seemed a bit scared. Cyrano sat patiently next to me.

"Your new family is here, Cyrano," Leonard said, taking the dog's leash.

"I'm going to miss that big guy," Meredith said. "Do you live in Fremont? With a dog?"

"I'm dog-sitting there," I said. I automatically reached for one of my business cards. I couldn't exactly hand one to Meredith when she was up to her elbows in water and soap.

She raised her eyebrows at me.

"Um, maybe you know him? I'm dog-sitting Elvis. He's a basset hound. A tricolored basset hound," I rattled off quickly. I didn't want to go into the whole thing about house-sitting and everything. Mom and I have to be careful who we tell. We don't want the schools to label me as a transient, because if that happens I won't be able to keep going to Cesar Chavez Middle School with all my friends.

"I think I know him," was all Meredith said.

Okaaaay...

"Does Elvis go to The Perfect Pet?" I asked. I don't know why, but the silences in this conversation were making me uncomfortable.

"Don't you know? I would think that a responsible dog sitter would know all of these details," she said. She had a hose in her hand, so I didn't want to say anything that would bug her.

"It sure seems like there are a lot of dogs in Fremont," I said. Why did I keep talking?

"Too many, if you ask me," she said.

That seemed like a weird thing for a dog lover to say.

"I don't know what you mean by that. Is there something wrong with Fremont?" I asked.

"There's nothing wrong with Fremont. It's a great neighborhood," she said. "I'm just not so sure that city dogs get the attention and exercise they need. I'm not convinced that any dog gets the attention and exercise it deserves. Every dog could use more walks."

Izzie's ears perked up at the word *walk*. So did mine. If we were in a cartoon, there'd be a thought bubble above Izzie's head with a person walking her down the street. There would be a thought bubble over my head with a lightbulb and dollar signs inside. I took this opportunity to pull out a business card.

"That's where I can help," I said. "I'm a reliable dog walker with good references."

Meredith took the business card and shoved it into the front pocket of her jeans without even looking at it. Then she looked at me. Intently.

"Keep a close eye on that basset. You wouldn't want anything bad to happen to him." She went back to rinsing Izzie.

What a weird thing to say.

CHAPTER 6

MOM PICKED ME UP RIGHT AFTER IZZIE'S BATH. I REALLY WANTED IZZIE to have the best home ever, but my gut ached every time I thought about not seeing her again. I know it's selfish. I tried not to get too emotional. Dogs can pick up on these things, and I wanted Izzie to be confident and happy when prospective new owners came to check her out.

Moms pick up on these emotional things, too. Mine put her arm around my shoulders as we walked to the car. I didn't even pay attention when she pointed the remote control key toward our Honda and clicked "unlock." But I had to smile as Elvis popped up in the front seat. This time I braced myself to stay steady when this drooling hound hurled his body at me.

"I'm never going to forget you, just like I'm never going to forget Izzie," I said, pushing his long wiggly body into the backseat of the car.

"I got the photo from Ted," Mom said. I'd offered to make a crisp black line drawing based on the photo of Boris. Mom thought it was a truly thoughtful idea and had called Ted to ask for a new photo. She handed me a framed picture of Boris, the bichon frise. "The photo on the flyer definitely didn't do him justice."

"I guess this means Boris didn't magically appear while I was at the animal shelter," I said.

Mom's silence was all the answer I needed. I pulled out my sketchbook and started drawing Boris. Drawing in a moving car isn't ideal, but I felt like I needed to do something. If Boris's owner wanted people to be on the lookout for him, it was clear to me that a better picture was needed on the flyer. Sure, the bright yellow paper and the word "Reward!!!" would get people's attention, but the photocopying process had turned Boris's fluffy white head into a muddy, blurry mess.

I kept working on the Boris drawing when we got back to the apartment. I wanted something unique about Boris to come through, but I needed to keep it simple enough so that it would copy well.

By three o'clock, I had it. I scanned the drawing and redesigned Ted's original flyer. Then I printed it on Piper's laser printer. Mom and I took it to Ted's apartment, 403, just down the hall.

"Did you say you're in middle school?" Ted asked. "That's hard to believe because this is so good. You really captured his personality, just from that photograph. It's uncanny." Ted was getting a little choked up. I would choke up, too, if my pet was missing.

"If it's okay with you, I could get this photocopied and we could put them up in the stores and restaurants around the neighborhood. We can go to all the same places where you put the flyer yesterday," I said. Putting up flyers would also give me an excuse to go into all the local shops, maybe even ask people some questions about the last time they saw Boris.

Ted seemed exhausted, and his voice was hoarse—probably from walking up and down the streets calling for Boris. He thanked me and handed me twenty dollars to make copies.

"I was wondering if you could tell me a little more about when he disappeared," I said. "Maybe I might find something because I'll have fresh eyes in the area."

"There's not much to say. He was there one second, gone the next. Boris was patiently waiting for me outside The Perfect Pet while I picked up—"

"The Perfect Pet?" I interrupted. "I thought the flyer said something about Joe's Special."

"I was inside Joe's Special picking up a clubhouse

sandwich. I'd called my order in earlier so I wouldn't be inside too long. I tied Boris to a metal post outside The Perfect Pet next door," Ted said.

"How was the leash secured to the post?" I asked, using my best inquiring-detective-wants-to-know voice. Ted grabbed a thin leash from his inside door-knob, looped it around a coatrack, pulled the hook end through the loop, and tightened it. It's the same way I'd secure a leash to a pole or a bench.

"The leash was gone, too," Ted said, confirming my suspicion. There's no way a dog could undo a loop that secure. If a dog had simply run away to follow a squirrel or to find food, the leash would have stayed behind.

"You know, my friends think I'm blowing this all out of proportion," Ted said.

"I don't think you are," I said.

He smiled in that way that says, That's nice of you, kid.

"Did you know that in most dognappings small dogs are taken," I said. I mentioned how the thieves go after small dogs, partly because they're portable but also because they're the hot dogs of the moment. "People pay a lot of money for small purebred dogs, and not all people care where the dogs come from," I said.

Uh-oh. I was getting that warning look from my mom again.

"I'm just sharing what I learned on the Internet..." I trailed off.

"I have a feeling you're on the right track," Ted said. "Small dogs are hot, as you say. Bichon frises are known as a highly desirable breed. Hypoallergenic. No shedding. Easy to train. Sweet and loyal."

No one had called to collect on the reward, which makes the dognapping-for-ransom scenario a little weaker. Yet it had been more than twenty-four hours since Boris had disappeared. That seemed to increase the chance that Boris was stolen. The dog thief might have already sold him for a ridiculous amount of money to someone who wanted a cute white dog as a fashion accessory.

"Thanks for all your help," Ted said wearily as Mom and I headed back down the hall. "I'm tempted to have you make one slight change and put the amount of the reward money on it. Perhaps that would help."

I was tempted to ask how much the reward was, but I didn't have to. Ted told me.

No wonder there were three exclamation points after "reward."

CHAPTER 7

"FOUR THOUSAND, TWO HUNDRED, AND FIFTY *DOLLARS*?" LILY PRACTICALLY screamed into the phone. "That is a huge amount of money."

"Exactly," I said.

"If someone knew that Ted would offer that kind of money, why didn't the dog thief just pretend to find the dog and collect the money?"

"Exactly," I said again.

"Suddenly this case is much more interesting."

"So now you agree that we have a case?" I asked.

I didn't quite catch what Lily said next. She was calling me on her mom's cell phone while they were driving from the Maple Leaf section of Seattle (my old neighborhood) to Fremont. Lily's dad, Dan, wanted to pick up some more organic vegetables at PCC. I'm not sure if the Shannons really needed to come to PCC, but they always go out of their way to make sure Lily and

I can spend lots of time together. It takes considerable more coordination now than it did when we lived down the street from each other, and I appreciated the effort.

It wasn't the money that made the case seem more real. Not directly, anyway. It was the fact that the amount of money was so large and still whoever had Boris hadn't tried to collect on it. But then again, people didn't know how big the reward was yet.

"We have to keep the option open that Boris is lost, plain and simple," Lily said. She was in our apartment looking at the flyer.

I gave her a look.

"Yeah, I don't believe it either. But it is still a possibility."

It was already four o'clock on Sunday afternoon. Most stores would close in an hour or two. We needed to get going if we wanted to hang the posters. Also, there was this little thing called homework that I'd successfully put off all weekend. I'd have to find time for that, too.

"Stop fiddling with that thing," Lily said. I was back at my laptop.

"Oh, I'm finished with Ted's flyer. I had another idea."

"Of course you did." Lily sighed.

"Here we go," I said, as Piper's printer spit out another flyer. Lily picked it up. She raised her eyebrows at me. "That's good thinking," she said.

"Let's go get them printed," I said, grabbing Elvis's leash.

"He's coming with us?" Lily asked.

"Of course. He's tracking Boris."

Lily rolled her eyes.

"You have to admit that he gives us an excuse to talk with people," I said. "He's our cover."

When we got to the copy shop, I gave Lily the choice of standing outside with Elvis or going inside to get copies made. Not surprisingly, she chose the inside job.

"Okay, make forty of each of these. Get the one for Boris on that same fluorescent yellow paper and get this other one on bright green."

"Well, hello, young Elvis." An elderly man walking down the street tipped his hat to us. He was the sixth person in five minutes to call Elvis by name. The man stopped and looked at the flyer that said Boris was missing. He made a *tsk-tsk* sound. "Such a shame, such a shame," he said.

"Here you go," Lily said, coming out with a stack of yellow papers and a stack of green. She pulled the old Boris flyer down.

"Now just a minute, young lady...Oh, I see," he said, as he read the new-and-improved flyer. "That is a much better likeness of Boris. You two must be helping Ted out."

This neighborhood was starting to feel like a small town in a movie where everyone knows everyone else's business. You'd think that would make it easier to find a dog. Whoever took Boris would have caught someone's attention. Sure, lots of people come to Fremont to eat and shop, but Boris was a local. They wouldn't just stand around while a stranger walked off with him. Unless the person who took Boris was also a local...

"I'm sorry, I didn't hear what you said." I realized that the man in the hat had continued talking while I was mulling things over.

He chuckled. "I was just saying that this is a fine idea," he said, nodding toward my green flyer that Lily had just taped to the window.

Does Your Dog Hate to Shop?
You'll get your errands done faster
if you leave your canine with me.
No more barking outside of shops,
no more worrying about
a tail-wagger breaking something inside a store.

Call for an experienced dog walker's help.

References available.

235-6628

I'd illustrated the flyer with cartoon scenes with Elvis, Mango, and Ruff, three of my star clients. Each vignette showed a happy dog walking alongside a responsible-looking twelve-year-old Chinese girl (me).

"Do you have a dog?" I asked.

"Me? No, I don't," he said. He sounded kind of sad. "I love dogs, but I'm afraid my wife was quite allergic. She was fine around cats, but sneezed up a storm around canines. I still have five cats. We had six at one time."

I noticed he talked about his wife and her allergies in the past tense. See? Always thinking. Always gathering information. Maybe this seemingly nice man was a crazy cat person. Maybe he actually hated dogs.

"I'm sorry," I said. I'd missed whatever he'd said. Again. Lily looked at me puzzled. He looked at me puzzled, too.

"I was saying that this is a fine idea, especially given recent events in the neighborhood. I'll be sure to spread the word. If people tell you 'Mack sent me,' you'll know it was me. That's me. I'm Mack." He tipped his hat again. It was one of those old-fashioned bowler hats, the kind that men wore with suits in old movies.

His seemed authentic, like he'd had it since the 1950s. "Good day," he said, and moved down the street.

"Nice man. Reminds me of my grandfather," Lily said.

Our next stop was Joe's Special. It was Lily's turn to go inside and my turn to stay outside with Elvis. I looked at the metal pole outside The Perfect Pet, where Ted had tied Boris's leash. It looked as secure as Ted said. Lily made a face at me through the restaurant window as she taped up our flyers.

"You might as well keep holding him because I'll just pop in here while I'm in the taping mode," she said. She turned the knob to The Perfect Pet, but it was locked. "Weird," she said. The sign was still turned to "Open." According to the hours painted on the door window, they were open another twenty-five minutes. I didn't think it would be polite to tape something to the outside of the shop's windows without their permission. Instead, I slipped two copies of each flyer through the mail slot next to the door.

Our final stop was Peet's Coffee, on the corner of Thirty-fourth and Fremont. I handed the leash to Lily.

"I don't see why we can't both go inside and Elvis can wait for us outside. No offense to the hound, but I don't think anyone would snatch him."

I glared at her.

"I mean, not that he's not adorable and wonderful. But he's rather heavy, so someone can't just pick him up and run. He's also rather vocal, and I think we'd hear about it if someone tried to take him," she said.

I glared at her again.

"What?"

"Ahem! The flyers?" I held up one of the green flyers. "It's completely counterproductive to leave Elvis outside when that's exactly what I'm trying to get people not to do."

"Oh...right. Unless you attached the flyers to Elvis's sides, and turned him into a walking outdoor billboard."

That comment didn't warrant a reply. I headed inside the coffee shop to ask if I could replace the "Missing" flyer and put up my green one. I pinned a copy of each on the bulletin board, and then taped two copies on the glass door—one on each side so that people would see them coming and going.

We ran out of flyers quickly. We should have made it to twenty different shops, but several shop owners wanted more than two copies of my green flyer. My friend Polly Summers at Capers, the one who introduced us to Piper, asked for extra copies and then said she was going to make even more herself. "I can quietly slip a flyer into certain customers' bags," she said. "Of

43

course, you and Elvis are always welcome in here. All well-behaved dogs are welcome. But I have to think that a dog might be a bit happier going on a quick walk with you than standing around here, especially when there are so many temptations here." I had to agree. Capers had some comfy-looking sofas and chairs for sale that might entice even the best-behaved dog to jump up and take a nap while his owner browsed.

"Did you hear about Ted's dog?" Two women carrying yoga mats walked through the door. My ears perked up. "Ted couldn't have been gone more than a couple of minutes and when he came out, Boris was gone," one woman said.

"I'm going to have to think twice before leaving Carly alone even for a second now," the other woman said.

"But it seems like it should be okay if you're just running in to get a cup of coffee or a gallon of milk," the other said.

Although I shared their sadness for Boris's disappearance, I have to admit I felt a little excited about my brilliant new approach to boosting my dog-walking business.

Mostly, though, I felt like *I* was lost, not Boris. I was completely lost about what to do next to find him.

CHAPTER 8

AFTER DINNER AND HOMEWORK, MOM PULLED SOME METRO BUS schedules out of her tote bag and spread them on the counter for me.

"I'm way ahead of you on this one," I said. I'm a master of Seattle's Metro buses, with at least fourteen route schedules imbedded in my brain. This time I had actually been a little stumped on how to get across town going west to east. I used Metro's online trip planner and had checked "fewest transfers" as my preferred route. Fremont might be the Center of the Universe, but getting to Cesar Chavez Middle School from there wasn't going to be that easy. "I take the 26 or the 28 downtown to Third, then transfer to the 14. I get off the bus at seven thirty-four and have eleven minutes to get to school, which should be plenty of time because Chavez is only two blocks from the bus stop. At the end of the day I reverse my route, taking the 14 downtown and catching the 26 or the 28. Piece of cake." I threw that last part in for added reassurance.

Mom gave me a big hug and a smooch. I know she constantly worries about me. I like to try to prove she can take it down a notch or two on the Worry Meter.

Monday morning went smoothly. Once again, my timing was perfect. The 14 pulled up just as I stepped off the 26. I made it to my locker and then to homeroom six minutes before the bell rang.

Mr. Park, my homeroom teacher, was trying to get one of those what-did-you-do-this-weekend conversations going. He looked at me.

"Um, not much. Just homework and stuff," I said, sliding down in my chair a bit, hoping he'd move on. He did.

Moving is a big deal, and almost anyone else in the world would have mumbled, "I moved." But Mom and I didn't want people—especially people at school—to know how often we moved. We couldn't risk some other parent challenging my right to go to Chavez since I didn't have a permanent address. A "right" permanent address, that is. Of course, we also didn't broadcast where we were house-sitting to protect the privacy of our clients.

Sometimes I use homeroom to race to finish last-minute details on homework. Sometimes I read. Today I was drawing Izzie and Elvis. Then I heard the word *Fremont*, and I snapped to attention.

"What did you do in Fremont?" Mr. Park asked Lily.

"Oh, you know. Just hung out. Hannah and I took her dog, I mean the dog of the people she's house-s…I mean dog-sitting." Lily was faltering, something that didn't happen that often. She sat up straighter as if collecting all her thoughts and going into Actress Mode. "We took a friend's dog for a walk around Fremont. I never really hung out there before. Do you go there, Mr. Park?"

Anyone who has been around Mr. Park for more than a day learns that all you have to do is ask him a question—instead of answering one of his questions—and you're safe from being called on for the rest of the day. He started talking about a summer solstice celebration, an outdoor film festival, the history of the Fremont area and the ship canal, the bus people statues, and the troll that lives under the bridge, and then the bell rang.

"We'll have to go back to Fremont sometime, okay, Hannah?" Lily said.

"Yeah. Right. Maybe this weekend," I said as we headed out to first period. Lily and I had endured an entire school year without having a single class, other than homeroom, together. We thought seventh grade would be our big chance because we each had four electives for the year. But Lily spent hers on jazz band and Spanish. I was using two electives to take Japanese all year, the third for advanced drawing, and the last one for animation.

Our school is huge, and the art room is on the exact opposite side of the school as Mr. Park's homeroom. I had to move fast to get there in time. Cesar Chavez Middle School is shaped like the letter U. Someone told me that if you went from one tip of the U to the other, it would be a quarter mile. I could go the interior route and get a quarter-mile walk in, or I could go out the back door of the school and cut across the garden, and then back inside to the hallway where the art rooms are. I always choose the outdoor route.

"I wasn't expecting this," said a voice next to me as we stepped out the back door. I know that Seattle has a reputation for raining all the time, but it doesn't really. Except now. It was a torrential downpour.

"Want to sprint?" I asked Jordan Walsh, the girl standing next to me. I knew Jordan was taking the same short cut—and not heading to one of the portable classrooms out back—because she's in my art class.

"Go!" she said, getting a split-second head start. But I made it to the other side of the garden first. I decided not to gloat about outpacing our school volleyball star. She might try to spike my head or something.

"Did you decide what to do for your theme?" Jordan asked as we got inside the art room. She was referring to our current art project. Our teacher, Mr. Van Vleck (he lets us call him V-2, as long as the principal isn't around) had given us an assignment he called "Studio Series 1." We were supposed to find a way to link a series of sketches together.

"I have no ideas," I said. "Do you?"

"No ideas. A big fat zero," she said, flopping her sketchbook onto the worktable.

There's nothing about Jordan that's a zero. She's tall, she's a great athlete, she's supersmart, and her family seems to have money to burn. I wouldn't say that Jordan and I are technically friends, but we keep getting thrown together in art classes and summer art camps. We also got thrown together last year when her mom was the toast of the town as an artist.

I opened my sketchbook and looked at what I'd done in the past few days. A picture of Izzie, a couple of Mango, one of Elvis, one of Boris, and another of Elvis. Dog doodles.

"Looks like you have a nice variety of subjects in your theme," Mr. Van Vleck said, glancing at my sketchbook.

I looked at him and at my drawings, then back at him, then back to my drawings. He'd already moved on by the time I squeaked out a "Thanks."

"And you said you didn't have any ideas," Jordan said.

"I didn't have any idea that I had ideas," I said truthfully. Once again, the answers were in my sketchpad. Apparently I'd selected dogs as my theme.

"You could do cats," I said. Jordan answered me with a "harrumph" noise.

I wish Advanced Drawing lasted all day. I like most of my classes, but I was happy to see the school day end. I walked out of the school and down the street to catch the Metro bus downtown. I got to the bus stop just as the 14 pulled up. I congratulated myself on my impeccable timing when it comes to Metro buses.

I climbed on board and settled into a seat near the window. Generally, I don't like it when people talk on their phones on buses, but it seemed acceptable to check my messages.

I had seven messages. "Whoa!" I must have said that out loud, because a woman across the aisle looked over at me. I gave her an apologetic shrug, and looked back at my phone. That many messages could mean that something was wrong, there was an emergency somewhere, there was someone who kept calling my number by mistake, or...my business was about to take off.

Fortunately, it was my business. It was booming. All seven callers inquired about my dog-walking services. Curiously, all seven callers also mentioned that Mack had sent them. Mack, that old crazy cat guy? Pretty nice of him.

CHAPTER 9

THREE THIRTY-ONE IN THE AFTERNOON, AND I WAS BACK IN FREMONT.
I called Mom as soon as I got off the 26 bus, and then
again when I got into the apartment. It's annoying to
have to call her so many times, but it helps me keep my
independence. This time she insisted that I wait until
she got home before I called back any potential new
clients. That was okay with me. I'd feel kind of stupid
calling now and saying, "Um, I have to ask my mom. I'll
call you back later." Not the kind of thing an entrepre-
neur would say.

I dumped my stuff on the kitchen table and grabbed
Elvis's leash. He couldn't wait to get outside. I walked
him down by the canal, and then we came back up
to the shops. The yellow flyers and the green flyers
were hard to miss. Every shop had them prominently
displayed. Except The Perfect Pet. That was odd. Maybe
they just hadn't put them up yet. Then I remembered

that they hadn't had Boris's first missing flyer hanging up either. Maybe they had a policy against taping anything up.

The bell rang as Elvis and I opened the door to The Perfect Pet. He barked—one deep, loud "woof" to announce our arrival.

Meredith, the volunteer I met at the animal shelter, came out to the counter. "Hi. I remember you said you were taking care of a basset hound," Meredith said. "Elvis is a regular here." Meredith seemed amped up today, especially compared to how she usually is at the animal shelter. I'd always thought of her as an extremely serious person. "You're Hannah, right? I'm good at dog names, usually, but I have a hard time remembering people's names. Now, Elvis has a card here, so we can give him a trim if you'd like."

I had no idea what she was talking about. "What do you mean by he has a 'card' here?"

"A nail card. You know," she looked at me expectantly. I must have returned a look that said, Huh?

"Elvis's owner, that tall, brown-haired woman? She pays in advance for nail trims for him. That way he can come in once every two weeks or so, and we cut his toenails. It's always important to keep a dog's nails short and trimmed, but it's especially important with a dog like this," she said. She lifted Elvis's front right paw. "See how large his paws are? There's a lot of weight that needs to be supported down here. The nails need to be cut or filed so that it's more comfortable for him. I'm surprised his owner didn't tell you all this. His file says that she's out of the country."

I sensed a tone of disapproval in Meredith's voice.

"I'm sure Piper, that's Elvis's owner, left all that information at home. I haven't gone through all of it yet," I said. Now Meredith's face wore a look of disapproval, perfectly in sync with her earlier tone. "I mean, I've gone through everything except the grooming information."

"Well, as long as you're here, we might as well trim those nails. It looks like it's been more than three weeks since he was last in. Really, he should be here every two weeks, three at the absolute outside." She looked at me expectantly.

"Okay. That would be great. What do I do?"

"You can stay here. We'll be right back."

I spent some time looking at tug toys, squeak toys, fetch toys, and chew toys. I think Piper had one of each model in a toy chest in her hall closet. She sure spent a lot of money on dog toys.

"Here's 'The King,'" Meredith said, using a nickname

that I guessed was a reference to Elvis Presley, since I knew some people called him "the king of Rock and Roll."

"Great. Thanks. I need to buy some of those, too," I said, pointing to a box with a dozen rolls of Doggie Bags. "I'm starting a dog-walking business," I added, just in case she was wondering what I needed with 240 poop bags. "And some liver treats, too."

Meredith sighed. I thought maybe she was upset that I was choosing plastic bags for picking up dog poop. But really, what else was I supposed to use?

"I just don't get these people," she said, letting out another big sigh.

"What do you mean?"

"Dog walkers, dog sitters. No offense. I don't get why people have dogs if they can't walk them and spend time with them. Making a commitment to a dog should be a major life decision," she said.

"I'm sure it is a major life decision," I said. It was something that I picked up from an article that my mom had printed out from the Internet. Usually I don't pay any attention to her stuff—I just pass it along when she forgets to pick it up from the printer—but this time the name of the article caught my eye. It was called "Getting Along Gets Easier," and at first I thought it might be one of those parenting articles about how to get along with your troublesome teen. I know, technically I'm not a teen yet, but that's not the point. I was relieved to see that it was actually about getting along with difficult coworkers. One of the tips in the article was to repeat and agree with a neutral statement the person just made.

Just to drive the point home, I paraphrased what she said. "A dog is a huge commitment. We owe it to them to take proper care of them," I said in a most earnest voice.

Meredith nodded.

Elvis started sniffing around a recycling bin. "Elvis!" I said, giving him a tug on his leash. His snout emerged triumphantly with a candy bar wrapper stuck to it. I bent down to take it from him, and my eyes caught sight of bright green and yellow paper.

"You never can tell what people will put in recycling," I said. "I hope there's nothing else in there that isn't supposed to be." I rifled through the recycling basket, as if I were looking for another candy wrapper. Sure enough, I found them. Not candy wrappers, but the yellow flyer about Boris and the green flyer advertising my dog-walking business.

Sketches

CHAPTER 10

"FIND ANYTHING ELSE DOWN THERE?" MEREDITH ASKED. SHE LEANED OVER the counter, her forehead and eyebrows scrunching up as she glared at me.

"Looks like the rest is all paper," I said, standing up. I couldn't figure out why someone would just toss those flyers aside. Unless...maybe it was good news.

"Do you know if anyone has found Boris?" I asked, but my voice was drowned out by Elvis's barking as the door to The Perfect Pet opened. A woman with a cinnamon-colored standard poodle—the biggest poodle—walked in.

"Well, hello to you, too, Elvis!" the woman said. Elvis immediately sat down and looked at her eagerly. He was in an I'm-a-good-dog-so-give-me-a-treat position. "Oh, you good boy. You want a treat, don't you?" She gave him a tasty reward.

"I'm sorry, I think I interrupted you," the woman said to me.

"Actually, I think Elvis interrupted me," I said. "I was just asking about Boris—"

"Such a sad thing, isn't it?" the woman said, this time really interrupting me. "We're all just worried sick about him. You probably saw the yellow flyer in our window." She turned to point to the window where, of course, there was no flyer. "Well, that's funny. I taped it up myself first thing this morning, and I'm sure it was there when I ran to PCC just now. Meredith, do you know where that flyer went?"

Meredith blushed. "No," she muttered.

"Boris is still missing," the woman said, turning her attention to me. "I just saw Ted at the grocery store. He's out of his mind with worry. Meredith, could you look up Ted's number? It's under 'B' for Boris. I'll need to call and tell him we need another flyer."

By now I'd caught on that this woman was the boss at The Perfect Pet.

"I helped Ted make the flyers, and I have some extras with me," I said, opening my messenger bag. I handed two to the woman. "Would you be willing to let me post my sign about my dog-walking business, too? I have references."

"Of course we can put that up! We had it up earlier, even though I didn't know who you were. I'm Arlene

Helm, the owner of the shop here." She held out her hand to shake mine.

"I'm Hannah West. My mom and I are taking care of Piper Christenson's apartment for a few weeks," I said. "And Elvis. We're taking care of Elvis, too." I found a business card and handed it to her.

"Good to meet you. It's strange. I don't know what happened to those flyers," Arlene said, as she rummaged through a desk drawer to find some tape. "I know Meredith here isn't a big fan of people needing to hire someone to walk their dogs." She found the tape and picked up the flyers to put them in the window. While she was in the front of the store, Meredith grabbed both the garbage can and the recycling can. She mumbled something about taking them out back. Arlene was still talking. Then she shook her head. "Some people are much more comfortable with animals than with other people," she said. I assumed she was talking about Meredith.

I looked over to the window. That same guy with Scooter the shaggy dog was outside studying the yellow flyer. The bell on the door clattered as my canine charge and I hurried outside. I don't know why, but it felt like such a relief to be out of there.

"Hey! Wait up!" I called out to Shaggy-Dog Guy, who had started walking down the street.

"What were you doing outside The Perfect Pet just now?" I demanded once I caught up with him.

"Scooter was getting water. Is that a crime?" I could tell from his voice that he was just joking.

Scooter sniffed me, and I scratched him behind his ears. "No, of course not. I just wondered why you were so interested in those signs. I thought maybe you had a lead on locating Boris."

"I was kind of hoping that Boris had been found already," he said. "See this poster for Boris? I noticed that it's different than the one that was up before. But I guess I'll keep looking."

"Are you hoping to get the reward money for Boris?" I asked.

"I wouldn't turn it down," he said. "But mostly I just want to help Boris. Do you know him?"

"Actually, no. Not yet, anyway. My mom and I met his owner. I helped him redo the poster. That one's mine, too," I said, pointing to the green one.

"That's cool."

"I'm Hannah, by the way. And I guess you already know Elvis."

"I'm Benito. But most people call me Ben," he said.

"You live around here?" I asked. I know that sounds totally corny, but I was in my detective mode of gathering information. "I thought you had to be in your twenties or thirties to live in Fremont."

"You live here. And you're not that old," he said. Crafty. He not only wasn't answering my question, he was turning it around. I decided to play along.

"I don't really live here. I just work here. You know, walking dogs and taking care of other things," I said.

"Do you go to Jefferson Middle School?"

"No. I go to Chavez." If I'd really lived in Fremont, I probably would be going to Jefferson. Elvis whined. He was done sniffing Scooter, and he wanted to get moving. "Apparently Elvis here wants to go up that hill."

"Scooter and I are going up to Market Time. I need a Snickers," he said.

Snickers! Any doubts I had about this guy immediately vanished with that one magic word.

"Are you kidding? Is there a place around here to buy real candy? I thought it would all be made of tofu and wheat germ or something," I said. The prospect of all that chewy nougat and caramel goodness covered in milk chocolate had me pretty excited.

"Haven't you been to Market Time yet?" he asked. I shook my head no. "I'll show you where it is. It's a big walk up the hill, but it's worth it. The owners are cool."

On the way up the street, Ben told me about the owners of Market Time. "They used to be hippies," he said, "but they're both total chocoholics. They can totally appreciate the need for a real candy bar."

When we reached the store, Ben and I took turns going inside so that one person was always outside with the dogs. Ben said he leaves Scooter outside all the time, and he thought it was perfectly safe. Still, I didn't want to take any chances. Especially since I was trying to get my new business off the ground.

It seemed like everyone in Fremont knew Ben, Scooter, or Elvis—or all three. But I got a few strange looks. I guess people were wondering what a stranger was doing with Piper's dog. Fremont is the kind of neighborhood where people look out for one another. Clearly that included looking out for dogs, especially since one had disappeared recently. People were curious about me, and even more curious once they found out that I was a legitimate dog walker taking care of Elvis. It actually turned out to be good for business. Having been hired by Piper was a great recommendation. But getting Ben's endorsement seemed like the best advertising of all.

"Are you the one who has the signs posted about dog-walking and pet-sitting?" a woman with a small wheat-colored dog asked.

I handed her my business card.

"Elvis is in good hands with Hannah," Ben said.

"I'll give you a call. I'd like to talk with your parents, too," the woman said.

And you can bet my mom is going to want to talk with you, too, I thought. And with everyone else who calls.

"I'll usually have Elvis with me, so I can walk your dog after school if your dog gets along with Elvis," I said again and again, handing out my business cards.

"How come you know so many people?" I asked.

"Everyone knows my grandfather around here, so they kind of end up knowing me, too."

We kept heading downhill, handing out business cards to anyone who showed any interest in my business. Some people who didn't even have dogs took one, telling me they were going to pass it along to a friend.

When we got back near the canal, I noticed Mack, across the street, talking animatedly with Ted, Boris's owner. They shook hands and then Mack tipped his hat. It seemed to be his trademark. Ted walked away, and Mack spotted us and waved from across the street. I waved back.

"Do you know Mack?" I asked Ben. "I see him everywhere."

Ben laughed just as my cell phone rang. No doubt it was my mom calling to remind me to get home and do homework. "Well," I told Ben, "Elvis got a longer walk than he expected. Now my mom—and my homework—are calling."

"See you later," he said. As I answered my phone, he crossed the street to talk to Mack in front of Costas Opa, the Greek restaurant on the corner of Thirty-fourth and Fremont.

CHAPTER 11

DID I SAY BUSINESS WAS BOOMING? I *SHOULD* HAVE SAID BUSINESS COULD potentially be booming. Although I had a bunch of calls about my availability as a dog walker, the Maggie West Inquiry System was holding me up. My mom wanted to talk to everyone first, and then she wanted to make arrangements for both of us to meet the canines and their owners. To further complicate it, I had ultimate Frisbee practice two days a week after school. Our school gets out superearly, so even with a two-hour practice and two buses, I could be home shortly after five o'clock.

We spent several days talking with dog owners and setting up times to meet that next weekend.

I was working on a new sketch of Elvis on Thursday night. He's a great model—a master at staying still. I had almost as many sketches of him as I had of Izzie. But I never got tired of sketching either of them.

I get kind of lost when I'm drawing. My sixth-grade art teacher told us it was "flow." She said it was this state of concentration when you have all this positive energy because you're enjoying yourself and you're totally absorbed in what you're doing. I'm not sure if I was totally lost in my drawing or in flow or what, but I seriously jumped when my cell phone rang and interrupted me. I didn't recognize the number, but the businesswoman in me decided to answer anyway.

"Hello, is this the number for the dog walker? I saw a flyer at Fremont Place Books," a woman said.

"Yes! That's me. I mean, I'm the dog walker. My name is Hannah West, and I'm extremely responsible. I've walked all kinds and all sizes of dogs, and I know a lot about dogs. I have references you can contact, if you'd like. Is there something I can help you with?" I was talking about a million miles a minute.

"Well, I normally walk Archie three times a day, but lately I've been getting home from work late, and I really think Archie would like some human interaction earlier than that. I'm actually looking for someone who could take him out in the mid- to late afternoon," she said.

"That's me! I mean, I can easily do that. I get out of school at two-fifteen, and I think I'll be home by three thirty or so. Would that work?"

"Oh, you're a student? Where do you go to school?" she asked. I figured this was a polite way of getting the information she really wanted to know: my age.

"I'm in seventh grade at Cesar Chavez Middle School. I walk dogs as an after-school and weekend job," I explained.

"I guess that might work. Could I check all this out with one of your parents?" she asked. I passed my phone to Mom, who talked *waaaay* too long with my new client. At last she handed the phone back to me.

"I didn't know you were staying in Piper's apartment," the woman, whose name was Nikki, said. "Elvis and Archie are great friends. I worked some things out with Maggie, and, if you're up for it, you could bring Elvis over here and pick up Archie and take them both for a walk after school. Everyone around here knows Elvis and Archie, so people will be looking out for you."

I completely forgot to ask what kind of dog Archie was. I'd be meeting him soon enough, because Nikki, my newest client, lived in the apartment building across the alley from us. Mom was taking me (and I was taking Elvis) over right away to meet Nikki and Archie, and to get a key and instructions.

I am happy to report that Archie is the sweetest bulldog that has ever walked on this planet. He and Elvis were excited to see each other. At least I think they were excited. If you know anything about bull-dogs and bassets, you know that they don't show a lot of emotion in their wrinkly faces.

When we got back to our apartment, Mom pulled out some paper and started mapping out a calendar. I'd agreed to walk Archie every day. Even the late walks on Tuesday and Thursday turned out to be okay with Nikki, who said they would allow her to stay down-town and take a yoga class before heading home. I'd walk him right after school on Mondays, Wednesdays, and Fridays, starting the next day, Friday. Then I'd meet all the other dogs and set up their schedules over the weekend.

I put Archie's apartment key on my key ring and into my messenger bag. Then I got everything ready for school the next day. I'm not the most organized person in the world, but I like to have things in order before I go to sleep. I crawled into bed with my sketchpad, quickly drawing Archie. I wasn't exactly in that flow zone my art teacher had talked about, but I was feeling pretty good. It turns out Archie was the missing link in my Studio Series for my drawing class. I had five dogs in a whole series of expressions and stances that I felt pretty happy about. I hoped Mr. Van Vleck would be happy about it. It's nice to be an artist, but it's even better to be an artist with good grades.

CHAPTER 12

"DO YOU ACTUALLY KNOW ALL THOSE DOGS?" JORDAN ASKED. WE WERE showing each other our plans for the Studio Series. "Or did you just check out a dog book and start drawing?"

"Yeah, I know them. I've taken care of almost all of them," I said, pointing out Izzie, Ruff, Mango, Elvis, and Archie. Okay, I hadn't actually taken care of Archie yet, but he was one of my clients. And helping Ted with the flyers for Boris was kind of like taking care of him.

"Do you actually know all those staplers?" I asked. For some reason, Jordan had chosen office supplies as her theme. You heard me: ordinary office supplies. Paper clips, a tape dispenser, a pencil cup, and more than a few staplers. I had to admit it was a rather brilliant idea. If I didn't like the way my dog series was shaping up, I'd wish I'd thought of something as commonplace as office supplies.

"All of my ideas led to dead ends. Then last night I was looking for a pencil sharpener in my dad's den. It took me a while to find it, but it was like he could open a stapler museum. Every drawer I opened had a stapler in it. It seemed kind of funny to me at the time. It's not as funny today," she said.

"I think it works," I said. "It's...different."

She snorted.

"Different is good," I added.

"*Riiiiight,*" Jordan said, stretching out the one syllable so it lasted about five extra beats. Lily and I had thoroughly analyzed Jordan over the past few months. She wasn't exactly the kind of girl who would think different was good, unless she was differentiated from the popular girls as being the *most* popular girl.

Mr. Van Vleck called us up one by one for quick conferences about our projects. He gave me eight out of eight points and told me to keep going. He spent longer with Jordan. She came back to the table looking relaxed and happy.

"What are you doing this weekend?" she asked, as we gathered our supplies at the end of the period. "You've got a game, right?"

"We have a game tomorrow morning. Then I'm spending some time with my dogs," I said. "How about you? Where's your game?"

"It's over at McKinley," she said. "Then I'm going to spend some time getting to know my staplers."

Was it possible that Jordan and I were becoming friends, I wondered.

Nah. We were just talking, finding common ground in our shared interest in art and sports—volleyball for her and ultimate Frisbee for me.

I kept thinking ahead the rest of the school day, anxious to get home to take Archie out for a walk.

And finally, at 3:33, I was back in Fremont. I dutifully called my mom when I got off the bus, when I got into the apartment (she insisted that I stay on the line while I got Elvis and his leash and left the apartment), when I got to Archie's apartment, and when I—finally—headed out with my two canine clients. All this calling is excessive, if you ask me.

For a short guy, Elvis was pretty strong. He practically pulled me across the alley and up the stairs to Archie's apartment. It was as if the two dogs hadn't seen (or sniffed) each other in ages.

It must have been pretty entertaining to see a bulldog and a basset walking down the street, because we got lots of attention. More attention than I like to get. I reminded myself it was the dogs, not me, that people were ogling.

I walked past the scene of the crime—Joe's Special. The bright yellow flyer for Boris and the green flyer for my business were still in the window. I wondered if that meant Boris hadn't come home in the time I'd been at school.

A noise startled me. Meredith was inside The Perfect Pet, rapping on the glass. She beckoned me in.

"This bulldog certainly looks familiar," she said in a singsong voice. "How are you, Arnold?"

"You're great, aren't you Archie?" I said, cleverly correcting her about his name without embarrassing her. Or so I hoped.

"Oh! I called you the wrong name, didn't I, little guy?" she gushed. Meredith was kind of hyper again. And she seemed a little too interested in Archie. It made me a little uncomfortable.

"Any news about Boris?" I asked, hoping to take the focus off Archie. When she didn't respond, I added, "The missing bichon frise?"

"Hmm? No. No news today. Did you know we do cat grooming here, too? We have special hours just for cats so they won't be stressed by being around dogs."

She kept prattling on. I had no idea why she was talking about cats or why she was talking so much in the first place. I find that sometimes it's best not to try making sense of what adults do when they act strange. I remembered what Arlene said about Meredith being better with animals than people. Maybe this is what she was referring to.

"Sorry. What?" I realized Meredith had finally stopped talking and was looking at me, as if waiting for an answer. Her eyes shifted, and I followed her gaze outside.

"I hope that missing dog is found soon," she mumbled in a sudden mood change. I had no idea what made her personality change so quickly. I looked outside again. Mack was in front of The Perfect Pet. He tipped his hat as if to say hello, and then wandered off.

CHAPTER 13

"IT'S PAYDAY!" MOM SAID, SWINGING THE DOOR OPEN AND INTERRUPTING my thoughts. Elvis immediately jumped down from the couch and went to the door for a belly rub. "Let's go to Blue C Sushi."

She didn't need to say anything else. Blue C was my absolute favorite restaurant, and living in Fremont meant it was just steps away. I pulled a hooded sweatshirt over my head and grabbed my sketchbook.

"Back soon," I said to Elvis.

Blue C Sushi means instant gratification. There's no wait to order or to get food. You sit at a counter and a conveyor belt a few inches above the counter carries little plates of sushi around the restaurant. If you see something you like, you grab it and put it on your tabletop. There's room for about forty people around the conveyor belt. I hoped we were early enough so we could get two spots together right away.

"Two of you?" the man at the door asked. Mom nodded, and he started to lead us to the counter. He stopped and said to her, "Does she need the green chopsticks?"

"No, she doesn't," I said, replying for my mom. Geesh. I hate it when adults don't speak directly to kids. They talk to your parent as if you're not even there. And I must say I was greatly offended that he thought I, of all people, would need the chopsticks that they give little kids (they're supposed to be easier to handle). I've been a chopstick master since I was four years old, and it's not just because I'm Chinese.

"Hey, listen, I'm sorry I did that," the guy said, this time speaking directly to me. "I hate it when people don't speak directly to kids."

This guy wasn't so bad after all, especially since he just said what was in my head.

"Now, remember we like green and yellow best. Especially green," Mom said, once we were seated.

I knew exactly what she meant. At conveyor belt sushi places, they figure out how much you owe for your food by counting your plates at the end of the meal. The plates are color coded for price. At Blue C Sushi, the yellow and green plates are the cheapest. If you avoided the dark blue plates, you could eat supercheap here. It was easy for me, because most of my favorites were also the least expensive. I went for the *kappa-maki* (rice and cucumber rolled inside seaweed; green plate) and spicy noodles (yellow plate). With tea, my dinner was less than five dollars.

"Doesn't that boy over there look familiar?" Mom asked.

I looked up from my sketch pad. He sure did. I knew the guy in the next seat, too. It was Ben and Mack. Were they together? I didn't think so. Ben looked like he was doing homework, and Mack was talking to one of the sushi chefs. I looked at the person on the other side of Ben. It was a man about my mom's age, who I assumed was Ben's dad.

My mom's friend, Lisa, came over to us. "Maggie!" she cried. "I heard you were house-sitting for Piper. And I heard you, Miss Hannah, are the talk of the neighborhood."

"What?" Mom asked, sounding a bit alarmed.

"I saw the signs advertising a dog-walking business, and one of my neighbors just handed me your card. She said she met you with Benito, up at Market Time." After that I tuned them out as they gossiped about former coworkers. I went back to sketching.

"I'll have Hannah call you to set up a time when

she can meet your dog," Mom said, nudging me with her toes.

"Right," I said, snapping to attention. "I'm very attentive and responsible."

Lisa and Mom said good-bye, and then Mom turned back to me. "Benito—is that the boy we met with the shaggy dog?" she asked. "I wish we knew a little more about him."

"Maybe we can go talk to him now," I said, but when we looked across to the other side of the counter, Ben was gone. So was the guy I assumed was his dad. Mack was just getting up, fishing some money out of his wallet to leave on the counter. He put his hat on and headed out, holding the restaurant door open to allow a group of older girls to come in.

"Oh, you guys! I found the most adorable teacup puppy on the Internet! He only weighs two pounds, and I think I'm going to get him!" one of the girls said.

"You *must* tell us the site where you found your dog," another girl said.

"I can't decide if I want a brown or a black dog," a third girl said.

"Black goes with everything," one replied.

"Brown is the new black." They all laughed. My *kappa-maki* suddenly felt heavy in my stomach. I couldn't believe that real people thought of their dogs as accessories. I thought that was just something you read about in magazines or see on TV.

We headed back to the apartment to get Elvis then took him for a walk together. We walked up the hill a couple of blocks. "Whoa! Where did that come from?" I asked, staring at a huge mansion up the street. It was such a surprise to see that big of a house in a neighborhood where it was mostly apartment buildings and businesses. The yard must have taken up at least half a city block. An iron fence ran around the perimeter of the property.

"I forgot about this place. I don't remember who owns it, but supposedly an eccentric old man and an army of cats live there."

A dog barked, and we heard a screen door close somewhere in the back of the house.

"I wonder how the army of cats likes that dog," I said.

CHAPTER 14

"I HAVE A SURPRISE FOR YOU IN THE CAR," MOM SAID AFTER MY FRISBEE game Saturday morning. I felt a total sense of déjà vu, like I was living last Saturday all over again.

My team, the Chavez Bulldogs, had just beaten Jefferson Middle School, the school close to Fremont where Ben goes. I didn't really expect Ben to be on their team, but I was kind of hoping he was.

"Is the surprise a drooling dog with droopy ears?" I asked.

"That's just a bonus," she said, unlocking the car trunk. She pulled a maple bar and a frosty blue Gatorade out of a grocery bag and handed them to me. "Great job, honey. I'm proud of you." She gave me a hug.

"And you're the best mom ever," I said, immediately taking a bite of the maple bar. I felt it was my responsibility to consume the pastry as quickly as possible before I got in the car and had to protect it from Elvis.

There was enough time for me to change my clothes before my volunteer shift at the animal shelter. I pulled a hooded sweatshirt over my head and changed from my cleats to regular sneakers.

"Hi, Meredith," I said as we practically collided in the doorway at the Elliott Bay Animal Shelter. She kept going, walking hurriedly to a blue car in the parking lot. I think the tires even screeched as she drove off, but that could have been in my head. She seemed to be in such a hurry that I imagined the tires screeching and gravel spurting out from under the tires.

"Hannah, can I see you?" Leonard asked as I was signing in. I followed him back to a small office. "I need to let you know that Izzie's gone."

I don't know what my face looked like, but it must have been pretty traumatized.

"No, no, no! I didn't mean it that way," Leonard rushed to say. "Gosh, I'm sorry. I just meant that Izzie has a new home."

"But that's a great thing! That's the best thing that could happen!"

"Of course it is. I just thought you'd be sad not to be able to see her today," he said.

I was sad, and I knew Leonard could tell that I was fighting back tears. Geesh! I wanted to kick myself for being so selfish. Our whole goal was to find good homes for animals.

"Did she—" I started.

"Yes," he said reassuringly. "She definitely went to a good home. A nice family adopted her. It was a good match all the way around."

"Thanks for telling me," I said. Leonard got up and started to head down the hall. "Wait!" I called after him. I opened my sketchbook and looked at the drawings of Izzie. I quickly reviewed them, and almost had to kick myself again for being selfish. I wanted to keep the best one for myself, but I forced myself to tear it from the book. "Here," I said, handing it to Leonard. "Do you think it would be possible to give Izzie's new family this picture of her?"

Leonard studied the drawing. "I'm sure they'll be honored and thrilled to have this," he said.

I met some great dogs during the next three hours, but I realized I was holding something back, as if I was afraid of getting too attached to one of them.

When my shift was over, I practically collided with Meredith in the doorway—again. Another déjà vu.

"We meet again," I said. I thought I was rather funny, but Meredith just barreled past me. Whatever.

At least Elvis was happy to see me. Once we got back to the apartment building after our walk, we took the elevator to the fourth floor. The doors were just starting to open when Elvis bolted, galloping down the hallway.

"Elvis!" I cried, running after him. I stopped when I saw what had him so excited. He was licking a little white curly-haired dog. A bichon frise.

"Boris?" I asked.

"Yes! It's Boris! I just got him back," Ted said.

"That's great! I'm so happy for you. When did you get him back?" I asked.

"Only about an hour ago." Ted picked Boris up. "I was just taking him for a little walk. I'm never letting him out of my sight again. Unless, of course, it's with a responsible dog walker like you."

"Will he let me pick him up?" I asked.

"Of course. He's as gentle and compliant as they get."

I picked up the white ball of fluff named Boris and cuddled him. He was absolutely adorable. He even smelled cute.

"He smells like you just gave him a lavender bath," I said, rubbing my nose in his neck.

"He is rather spotless, now that you mention it. He doesn't seem to be affected by what happened, either. He's calm and happy."

"Where was he? How did you get him back?" I asked.

Suddenly Ted, who'd been chatty and relaxed just a moment ago, was in an ultra rush. He scooped Boris out of my arms. "Oh, that doesn't matter," he said hurriedly. "The important thing is that he's back. Gotta go!" he called, heading toward the elevator.

Was I imagining it, or was he avoiding my question?

CHAPTER 15

MOM HELPED ME WORK OUT DOG DETAILS OVER THE WEEKEND. SHE finished prescreening all my clients—the human clients—and took me to meet each dog and its owner. Archie and Elvis were the only ones getting a walk every weekday. But I had plenty of other dogs on all the other days; some were just once a week, some twice, and others three times a week.

"I hope you can still fit me into your busy after-school schedule," Lily said on Wednesday morning, looking down at the calendar Mom had helped me set up. "Let's see, I can squeeze you in right after school, but I've got Archie, Sadie, and Otis this afternoon, too. Not to mention Elvis."

"Wow. How many canine clients do you have now?" Lily said, trying to make sense of the rather complicated schedule I had. Each day had the names of the dogs who needed walks, and each dog had an entry with the owner's name, address, phone number, and what kind of exercise the dog needed. "Is Elvis going to be able to keep up with you?"

"It's a myth that bassets are lazy and fat. They actually have incredible endurance. Elvis could walk twenty miles a day if he had his way. He has no problem keeping up. In fact, you might have a problem keeping up with him."

She rolled her eyes at me. "I'll meet you at your locker," she said, fishing a Metro bus ticket out of her pocket and then stuffing it back in again.

After school and two bus rides, Lily and I dropped our things in Piper's apartment and took Elvis down the hall to pick up Sadie, a cocker spaniel. Next stop was Archie's.

"We need to pick up one more after this. You can take two dogs and I'll take two dogs," I said.

We went and got Otis, a gray miniature schnauzer from the same building where Archie lived. We took the dogs to the path by the canal first, so they could sniff and do their business. Then Lily wanted to walk around the shops, so we headed back.

The dogs took a communal drink at the dog bowl in front of Joe's and The Perfect Pet.

"Is that store ever open?" asked Lily, nodding toward the "Closed" sign in the window of The Perfect Pet.

"Of course it's open. Sometimes, that is," I read the sign with its hours. "It just doesn't appear to be open when it says it will be."

"Let's take all the dogs home and then see what kind of snack food your mom bought," Lily said.

I was about to tell her that my mom's idea of junk food these days wasn't exactly in line with the needs of two hungry girls, but I didn't get a chance to say anything.

"She's gone!" a woman screamed. "She...just... disappeared."

CHAPTER 16

ABOUT A HALF-DOZEN PEOPLE GATHERED AROUND THE WOMAN OUTSIDE A store called London's. I had to stand back a bit because I had a dog—or two—with me. Unfortunately, the woman who screamed didn't have a dog with her. That was the problem.

"I just went back to my car to get my glasses out of the glove compartment. I left Daphne right here because she seemed so content," the woman said, practically hyperventilating. "When I came back, she was gone. I called for her a few times, but someone must have taken her. Her leash is gone, too."

Elvis barked, which startled everyone. He pulled at the leash, wanting to go down Thirty-fourth Street. He somehow signaled Archie and the other two to start pulling as well. I held my ground.

"Excuse me," I said through the crowd. "What kind of dog is Daphne? We can help you look for her."

"She's a pom-poo—you know, a Pomeranian-poodle mix."

I could sort of imagine what a dog like that might look like, but not exactly. "Do you have a picture?" I asked.

"Of course," the woman said. She pulled a photo out of her wallet. Mack, the old guy in the bowler hat, took it from her. He looked intently at the photo, nodding. He passed the photo to the next person, and it finally made its way to Lily and me. A little brown speck of a dog was pictured with a shopping-mall Santa. "Daphne is about eight pounds. She's tan with dark brown markings. She has a brown spot around one eye and a brown tip on one ear. She's absolutely adorable. Oh, what am I going to do? I need to stay here in case she comes back, but I need to look for her, too."

"Oh, Jennifer, this is so horrible. Just like when Boris disappeared," a man said.

"Boris made it back safely, though," Lily said.

"We can help you look right now," I offered.

The woman looked at me skeptically. I told her I'd made the flyer for Ted and that I'd be happy to do the same for her. She gave me another skeptical look.

"I know Ted offered a big reward," she said. "Even though she means the world to me, I'm not sure I can do that."

"I don't think reward money will be necessary," Mack said.

"But it couldn't hurt," Lily added.

The woman wrote down her name and phone number for me, and I handed her my card.

There was a chorus in the background of people calling for Daphne.

"Daaaa-phneee! Daaaa-phneee!"

"Heeeere, Daphne! Come here, girl!"

"What if she's trapped somewhere?" Lily whispered.

"We'd probably hear her bark or whimper," I said.

I had a feeling I'd be making another flyer that night.

CHAPTER 17

TWO MISSING DOGS IN LESS THAN TWO WEEKS. A COINCIDENCE? I DON'T think so. There were too many things in common. Both were little dogs. Portable dogs. Each weighed less than ten pounds. Someone could pick either one up and tuck it under a coat or into a bag and just walk away. Someone could even run away because the dogs were so small.

Each time the owner had been just steps away from the scene of the crime. Conceivably, the dog owners could have come back at any time, interrupting the crime. Unless the dognapper knew the owners' habits so well that the dognapper could anticipate how long the owner would be gone.

I wanted to know more about pom-poos. After Lily and I ate all the soy nuts and pears in the house, she headed home and I headed for my laptop.

Pom-poos are sometimes called pomapoos or

pooranians. This mixed breed was half toy poodle and half Pomeranian. Crossing dogs with poodles seemed to be getting more and more popular. Last summer I'd taken care of a wonderful Labrador/poodle mix—a labradoodle—named Mango. In the small dog world, people were going poo crazy. There were yorkie-poos (Yorkie and poodle), shih-poos (shih tzu and poodle), schnoodles (miniature schnauzer and poodle), cock-apoo (cocker spaniel and poodle), and many other dogs with a "poo" tacked onto their mix. I was momentarily distracted by a Web site that advertised "Designer Dogs," where people were offering chugs (chihuhua and pug mix) and pugles (pug and beagle mix).

Designer dogs? I flashed back to the college-aged girls I'd overheard at the sushi restaurant. They'd been talking about choosing a dog based on what color would look best with their outfits. "Brown is the new black," one had said. They'd also said they were shopping for dogs on the Internet, as if the dogs were shoes you'd order from an online store.

Designer dogs also made me think of celebrities carrying small dogs around as if the dog were a fashion accessory. It turns out that there are dog fashions just like there are clothing fashions. When I was little, dalmatians were all the rage because of a movie (I think you can guess which one) featuring the white dogs with black spots. A few years later, pugs were superpopular based on a movie with a pug named Frank. Chihuahuas and teacup dogs all became popular because of movies, TV, or celebrities.

Now there was a booming business of shifty people selling little dogs on the Internet. You could buy a dog without ever meeting it. The dog would then be put on a plane and sent to you. I could see that there was some serious money in dealing little puppies. But would people pay as much for a full-grown dog? Pugnapping seemed to be a popular endeavor for crooked canine thieves. If you have a pug, you can't even leave him or her in your front yard to romp freely because someone could reach over the fence, pass the pug to a partner in a pickup, then speed away.

Boris and Daphne were even more portable than pugs. They had a high price on their heads if sold. And, of course, there was the substantial reward money Ted had offered for Boris's safe return.

It was getting late, especially for a school night. Mom was still downtown working at Wired Café. A beep told me I had a new e-mail. It was from Ben. I had given him my e-mail address so he could let me know about any potential clients he might have for me.

Did you hear that another dog is missing? My grandpa says it's a little white Pomeranian named Daphne. You should make another flyer. If you want, that is.

Scooter says "hi."

See you later.

Ben.

I had had a feeling I would be making another flyer, but so far Daphne's owner hadn't called me. I checked my cell phone to make sure it was on. But guess what? It wasn't.

I had fourteen new messages. Only one of them was from Jennifer.

CHAPTER 18

"EVERYBODY THINKS I HAD SOMETHING TO DO WITH IT!" I WHINED TO mom when she finally got home.

"I doubt that's true. Why don't you let me listen to the messages?"

I handed my cell phone over to her. She took notes as she listened to each message.

"Well—" she started to say.

"They think, since we're new in the neighborhood, that I'm using my dog-walking business as a cover to get close to the dogs," I said.

"I'm not sure that's true..." Mom said.

"Then why did all my Thursday and Friday clients cancel?"

"They didn't all cancel. You still have Archie. And Elvis, of course."

"But the others? They don't think they can trust me," I said. I wasn't sure if I was mad or sad. Both, I decided. I was definitely mad that people would jump to conclusions, and I was sad that those conclusions implicated me as having something to do with the two missing dogs.

Okay, so no one came right out and said: "We've seen you around the neighborhood with dogs that aren't yours. You seemed to appear right about the time that the dognappings started. You obviously have something to do with it, and we absolutely cannot trust you with our pets."

"Hannah, listen to me," Mom interrupted the tirade in my head. "People are just saying they're worried about their dogs. They sounded genuinely concerned for you, as well. If someone is really dognapping these dogs, they certainly don't want a young girl to be in the middle of it. After listening to those messages, I don't want you in the middle of it, either. You could get hurt."

This time it was my turn to listen to the messages again. People were worried about their dogs and didn't want them out of their sight. But I still think two or three people had a tone of voice that was a bit accusatory. New girl arrives; dogs disappear. Never mind that Boris disappeared hours before we moved in. Or that he'd been returned.

Speaking of which, I asked Mom if she'd heard

anything from Ted about where Boris had been or who collected the reward money.

"I've run into him a few times, but he's always on his cell phone," she said. "Come to think of it, a couple times he pulled the phone out when he saw me. Of course, it could have just rung."

I'd used that trick to avoid talking to people several times myself.

For some reason, Ted didn't want to tell us the details about Boris's disappearance and return. Granted, we weren't old friends or anything, but why would he pointedly avoid talking about it?

I told myself that it was good that business had slowed down, although "screeched to a halt" would be a more accurate way to phrase it. I had an ultimate Frisbee tournament on Saturday that involved teams from half of Washington State. In fact, I was going to have to skip volunteering at the animal shelter this weekend. And, of course, there's always that little thing called homework.

Still, it was pretty depressing to think that my business had blossomed and died in the space of about forty-eight hours. I was down to just two dogs to walk after school on Friday. I called Nikki to make sure she wanted me to walk Archie.

"Absolutely. He loves your after-school walks," she said. "Unless you don't want to walk him anymore." She sounded worried, as if I might not like her dog.

"I love walking Archie. It's just that, well, honestly, a few of my clients have canceled. I think they're worried about the dognappings," I said. "I mean, they have every right to be worried. But I don't see how canceling an exercise date for your dog with someone as responsible as I am can help keep your dog safe. I just want to be sure that you feel okay leaving Archie with me."

Nikki laughed. "You don't have to sell me on how responsible you are. To tell you the truth, all dog owners in the area are a little freaked out. I feel like more than ever I need someone who will keep an eye on my Archie. Don't let people freaking out freak *you* out."

Nikki told me she'd set up an account with The Perfect Pet. "If you feel like taking Archie in for a nail trim one of these days, that would be great."

I put the finishing touches on a flyer for Daphne and e-mailed it to Jennifer. She was going to copy it and put it up right away, before people headed out to work the next morning. By the time I headed to the bus stop to catch the 28, there were orange flyers advertising Daphne's disappearance in the places that Boris's flyer once occupied. As my bus pulled away, I caught a glimpse of Jennifer coming out of Peet's Coffee with Mack. They shook hands, and he did his customary tip-of-the-hat gesture.

My cell phone vibrated almost immediately. I don't like to talk on the phone when I'm on a bus, but I recognized Jennifer's number.

"Hello?" I whispered, trying to be discreet.

"It's Jennifer. Are you still at home? I need to make a change to the flyer," she said. "It's imperative that we make it clear that there is a significant reward for Daphne's return."

I resisted the urge to ask how much "significant" equaled in terms of dollars, but not only was that none of my business, it wasn't actually important. It's just interesting that she'd so sorrowfully said the day before that she couldn't offer a cash reward. In fact, she'd said that maybe she could scrounge up "fifty dollars or so after the weekend." Why the sudden change? Had she sold a family heirloom or something?

I told her I was already on a bus heading downtown.

"That's okay. I have a pen with me. Maybe I'll get more attention if I add the note about the reward in handwriting."

"I could do it after school," I offered.

"No, thanks. I need to do it now. Ted made it pretty clear to me that the only way he got Boris back was because of the cash reward he offered. I've got to get started," she said. "Thanks."

She hung up.

Had Boris really been dognapped? Had the dognappers threatened to snatch him again? Maybe that's why Ted was being so secretive about Boris's return.

I was glad he could give Jennifer some advice that might get her dog home sooner.

CHAPTER 19

IT RAINED ALL WEEKEND, WHICH MADE THE ALL-DAY FRISBEE TOURNAMENT on Saturday a little less fun. But only a little less, because it was still superfun to get to play five games in one day. Winning four of those games added a little bit to the fun factor.

Mom had the weekend off to watch my games and spend what she called "downtime" with me. Thanks to the steady supply of Seattle rain, we spent most of that downtime inside.

By Sunday night, there was still no news about Daphne, even though Jennifer had made it abundantly clear that a reward was being offered. "Substantial REWARD!!" was written in bold, black marker on each of the orange signs.

Maybe money wasn't the answer.

After dinner on Sunday, Mom and I took the dog out for a short walk, zigzagging our way back and forth through the main Fremont streets. We stopped at the steps of the Lenin statue for Elvis to do some extra sniffing. Having a statue of a former Communist leader on display as public art was controversial at first, but the general consensus now was that it was a beautifully crafted statue that ignited some healthy political conversations. At least that's what I read in the History of Fremont Web page.

A familiar-looking woman sat on a nearby bench, holding a red umbrella. I think she jinxed the weather because all of a sudden it started dumping rain.

"Let's get home!" Mom said. But Elvis took that exact moment to stop and, as they say, "do his business." I waited patiently (or not so patiently) for him to finish, but Elvis was taking his time.

As we watched, a man in a yellow rain slicker and matching rain hat approached her. The woman with the red umbrella stood up, and I thought again there was something familiar about her. The man reached out and they shook hands quickly. Then the woman stuffed her hands into her pockets, and the man quickly tucked his hands under his arms. Weird. Were they just trying to stay dry, or was there something else going on? The woman turned quickly, then scurried away in the rain. The man in the slicker looked toward us. I couldn't see his face because his hat was pulled low. But I did see him reach up and move the brim up and down in one smooth motion, as if tipping his hat.

"Was that Mack?" I said, voicing my thoughts out loud.

At the same time, Mom said, "If I didn't know better, I'd say that looked like a ransom drop."

The word *ransom* made me think of Jennifer and her urgency about the reward. Suddenly I realized why the woman with the umbrella had seemed familiar. I was pretty sure it *was* Jennifer.

There was a loud clap of thunder, and it started raining even harder. Part of me wanted to stay to figure out what was really going on, but the more rational part of me was busy concentrating on getting out of the rain as quickly as possible.

Back in Piper's apartment, we sat at the kitchen counter drying off and sipping warm cups of peppermint tea. Mom refused to listen to my theories about the dognapping case. She was too busy enjoying the fact that someone named Mack was wearing what she called a "mack." She said that was the word Brits used for a rubberized rain jacket. She started singing a song I recognized from the Beatles.

Parents are so easily amused. And so weird.

I went to bed, but I couldn't stop thinking about Mack and Jennifer.

That Wednesday, Lily came home with me after school. It was raining again, but this time it was a light rain, the kind of rain we get most often in Seattle. It's not enough to deal with the hassle of an umbrella, but it's a constant drizzle that's less than pleasant. Elvis and Archie were with us, and, true Seattle dogs that they are, they didn't seem to mind the rain.

"Let's walk under the bridge for a ways to stay drier," Lily suggested.

"Whoa! I didn't know he was going to be right here! I remember him totally freaking me out as a kid," I said, as we walked toward the famous Fremont Troll. I hadn't been to see it since we'd lived there, and it wasn't because I was still scared. I had promised Mom that I wouldn't go under the bridge alone, just in case an unsavory sort was hiding under there, but I don't think she meant this piece of public art.

"He's not as scary close up as he used to be," Lily said. "He's actually almost cute. I was petrified of him when I was little."

I thought he still seemed pretty scary. The Fremont Troll is one of the more famous outdoor sculptures in the area. He's pretty impressive, this shaggy-haired troll who seems to be crawling out of a cave under the bridge. He's massive, but all you can really see is his craggy face and his enormous hands, one of which is crushing a real, honest-to-goodness Volkswagen Beetle. Not a replica of a Beetle, but a real car. When we were little, Lily and I used to dare each other to walk on the troll's arm or touch his nose. Lily was right, though. He is kind of cute now, if you like the idea of a creature crushing a car.

"Yo, Elvis! Over here!" Ben called from the other side of the troll's hulking left arm.

"Who's his little pal?" Lily asked.

She wasn't talking about Scooter. Because walking on a leash next to Scooter was a little dog.

I was pretty sure the little pal was Daphne.

CHAPTER 20

"IS THIS...?" I STARTED TO ASK.

"Absolutely. It's Daphne. My grandfather asked me to take her for a walk. I'm Ben, by the way," he said to Lily.

"I'm the sidekick, also known as Lily."

"How in the world did your grandfather end up with Daphne?" I asked.

"I'm not exactly sure. But like I told you, Grandpa knows everybody. I think Jennifer asked him to keep an eye on Daphne while she went back to work."

"What did you find out about Daphne? How did Jennifer get her back? Where was she? What's the story?"

"I don't know exactly. All I know is that Jennifer said she didn't know what would have happened if she hadn't been able to come up with the same reward money as Ted," Ben said.

Yeah, the money that I saw her give to Mack last night, I thought bitterly. But I didn't want to say anything about the case until I had more evidence. So all I said was, "You didn't ask?"

"Uh-oh," Lily said under her breath. "When you hang out with Hannah, it's pretty much understood that you have to constantly assist with her cases."

"Cases? What are you talking about?" Ben asked.

"There's obviously a connection between the way the two dogs disappeared. Maybe there's a connection in the way they were returned," I said, talking a mile a minute. "But we don't know that because no one is giving us any details on who returned the dogs or how they were returned."

We walked back down the hill, with the three dogs leading us to their favorite water dish in front of The Perfect Pet.

"Maybe my grandfather knows what happened. I bet he can tell us something," Ben said.

We let the dogs finish their drinks, and then Ben started to lead Scooter down the street. "Let's go over to Costas Opa," Ben said.

"Is it time for a lunch break?" Lily joked. "Maybe we should go to Norm's so we can bring the dogs with us." I had told Lily about how the restaurant actually encouraged dog owners to bring their furry friends in with them. I couldn't tell if she believed me, or if she was testing Ben to see if I'd made the whole thing up.

But Ben just laughed and shook his head. Before I could ask him why we were really going to Costas Opa, the door to the restaurant opened and Mack walked out.

"Benito, my boy! Why don't you walk an old man home?" he asked.

"Sure, Grandpa," Ben said.

Then Mack turned to us. "Nice to see you, girls," he said. Then, of course, he tipped his hat. He always does that. But this time I couldn't smile in response. I was too dumbfounded.

"What's wrong with you?" Lily asked. I was still staring as Ben, his grandfather, and the two dogs all walked back up Fremont Avenue.

"I didn't know that was his grandfather," I said, feeling incredibly stupid. Ben was always talking about how his grandpa knew everyone. I'd seen him at least twice with Mack. How clueless could I be?

"How clueless can you be?" Lily asked for me. "I can't believe you didn't know that."

"You mean you knew that Mack was Ben's grandfather?" I asked, a bit surprised.

"Of course not! How would I know that?" Lily said with an exasperated tone. "But you're a detective. You're supposed to notice details like family relationships. But that doesn't matter, does it?"

Lily was right. At least on one account. I *should* have realized it sooner. I couldn't believe that I hadn't made such an obvious connection.

But on the other hand, she was wrong. It *did* matter. How would Ben feel if his grandfather turned out to be a dognapper?

CHAPTER 21

BY FRIDAY I STILL HADN'T PICKED UP ANY OF MY OLD CLIENTS. BOTH Boris and Daphne were home. No other dogs were missing. Yet people were still skeptical about me and my ability to take care of their dogs. Mom kept telling me not to take it personally. It was natural for them to worry about their pets.

"They aren't accusing you of anything," Mom said. "But they might be worried that their pets will be more vulnerable if they're with someone else."

Someone like Mack? I thought bitterly. But even though I had some strong suspicions about him, I couldn't prove that he had done anything. And no one else seemed to be worried about him at all.

Archie was a loyal client. On Friday, Elvis and I picked him up and brought him to The Perfect Pet. This time I was solo. No Lily. No Ben.

"And how are Elvis and Archie today?" Mack asked when I ran into him outside the door. He bent down to pet each of the dogs. "I'm glad to see these two getting extra walks in the daytime. Not good for an animal to go all day without a walk. Not good for humans to go all day without a walk, either." He tipped his hat and headed south on Fremont. I watched as he headed toward the canal. I had a pretty good idea that he was going to Costas Opa.

"Is Meredith working today?" I asked as I walked into The Perfect Pet. Arlene, the owner, was at the counter, and her poodle, who I'd learned was actually named Cinnamon, lay on a small mat on the floor next to her.

"She called in sick today," Arlene said, with obvious irritation in her voice. "Terrible time to be short staffed. Fridays are always busy. But we can always squeeze in nail trims for these dignified gentlemen."

"Only for Archie, the bulldog. Meredith just trimmed Elvis's nails."

I helped lift Archie onto the table. Arlene talked to him gently the whole time, telling him what a good boy he was. I helped distract him when she was working on his front paws.

"I hope Meredith is better tomorrow. We both volunteer at Elliott Bay Animal Shelter on weekends," I said. I'd missed last weekend and was looking forward to working at the shelter again.

"Sure, Meredith calls in sick to work, but she'll go off and donate her time to homeless animals," Arlene said.

I could tell she was more than a little ticked off. I decided to use the agreement technique to get her talking more. "It must be so hard to run a business under the best circumstances, but extraordinarily hard when an employee is sick."

"It sure is hard," Arlene agreed. "It's even hard sometimes when she is here. Nothing's wrong with Meredith's work, but her attitude is terrible. It seems like she's angry at the dog owners who live around here. And lately she's been acting as if she doesn't even need a paying job."

Arlene's last comment made me think. I knew Meredith didn't get paid for her work at the shelter. So if she was acting like she didn't need to get paid at The Perfect Pet, that could mean that she was getting money from somewhere else.

Arlene's voice interrupted my thoughts. "Okay, Archie. You're ready to dance away the weekend."

I helped Archie down, and we went outside, where Elvis immediately started barking. At what, I don't know. Have I mentioned that when a basset hound barks, it's extremely loud? Once Elvis got going for a while, he'd lift his head to the sky and start howling.

People called it a basset bray, but it sure sounded like a howl to me.

"Hannah!" Elvis stopped howling when Ben called my name. I wasn't used to seeing him without Scooter by his side. Elvis and Archie seemed disappointed.

"Where's Scooter?"

"I can't find him." Ben looked seriously distressed.

"Oh, no! Was he stolen?" Scooter was adorable, but he didn't fit the profile of the little cute dogs that had been snatched in the past week.

"I, I don't know. I've looked all over for him, but I can't find him anywhere. Can I use your cell phone to call my grandfather?"

I tried not to eavesdrop as Ben filled Mack in on the situation. Then Ben handed the phone back to me, saying, "My grandfather wants me to come home so we can figure out what to do. Can you come? Maybe you can help make flyers or something."

I told Ben I'd need to call my mom and ask for permission. She wanted details, like she always did: address, phone number, and all that. I handed the phone to Ben and he rattled off a bunch of numbers. Mom said she'd let Nikki know that I was keeping Archie for a while longer.

Ben and I practically raced up the street. Then up another. We were going up the steep hill and onto the street where that eccentric old guy is supposed to live. The wind kicked up a few notches, and the tree branches started whipping around. It made the huge beautiful house look old and creepy, just like a movie.

"You live here?" I asked Ben, amazed. He was opening the massive iron gate at the front of the property.

"In the back," Ben answered. "Come on."

My mind whizzed. First, I hadn't realized that Mack was Ben's grandpa. Now it turns out that Ben lived behind the mansion. Did that mean he knew the eccentric rich guy?

I followed Ben to the back of the house. Stone paths meandered through the back of the property, passing a fountain and a pond. Potted plants lined the edges of a stone patio. I had expected to see a smaller house in the back, but Ben opened a screen door and then a heavy wood door that led inside the mansion. He headed up an inside staircase to the right.

"This is where you live?" I knew there were important things to discuss, but I was in a temporary state of shock. We'd entered a light-filled room that stretched from the back of the house to the front. On one end, two large couches faced each other on either side of a stone fireplace. Another corner had two oversized chairs and ottomans, surrounded by books. Through an arched doorway was a formal dining room, the kind

I've seen only in movies and on TV. The kind where you could easily seat twenty people for dinner and then the butler and the maid would come in and serve you a five-course meal. "You live *here*?" I asked again.

"Just the upstairs part. Grandpa had it converted when we came to live here. Dad and I live on this floor. Grandpa has the first floor, but he spends most of his time up here with me and Dad. Come on."

"Is it okay for the dogs to come?" I asked.

"Of course it's okay. Hurry."

Elvis had bolted up the stairs. Archie followed along as well, but he needed some coaxing.

The kitchen was large, but I could tell it wasn't fancy-schmancy. This looked like a kitchen where people really cooked and talked and ate. Mack was at the stove, but he turned around when we walked in.

"Sit down and have some cocoa. And then we'll figure out what we need to do," Mack said.

"Grandpa, can I go back out? I want to keep looking around for Scooter," Ben said. "You and Hannah can decide what to put on the flyers." His grandfather gave him a hug and wished him good luck.

"Maybe I should go, too," I said. I wasn't so sure that I wanted to be alone with Mack.

But Mack stopped me. "Please stay," he said. His

is behind all this. The only thing that matters to me now is getting Scooter back home where he belongs."

I did have an idea who was behind it. Especially now that I was sure it wasn't Mack. I filled him in on my theory.

Mack instructed me to take Archie and Elvis home, and then go help Ben search for Scooter. He also said not to follow him.

I half listened to him. Ten minutes later, I found Ben walking up and down Fremont Avenue, calling Scooter's name. I told him that I'd check over on Thirty-sixth Street. Something in my gut was telling me that Mack was on his way to the Lenin statue.

On the way over there, I was silently willing Archie and Elvis to be quiet. Mostly Elvis. I guess dogs really are intuitive, because they were both perfectly quiet, they sat motionless when I stopped, and they walked easily beside me when I walked. They were the best dogs ever, and I promised myself I'd give them extra treats when we got home.

I neared the Lenin statue, and sure enough I spotted Mack. Did the dognapper know this was where Mack had met Jennifer? Or was it just the most obvious meeting place? I made sure that Mack couldn't see me, and I watched to see what would happen.

voice was so gentle and so full of concern for Ben that all my worries went out the window. How could I ever have thought that Mack had anything to do with the dognappings?

"I have some things I want to tell you. But first, I have a feeling you might have some questions for me, Hannah, so please feel free to ask. But don't let your cocoa get cold."

Boy, did I ever have some things to ask. As is often the case, my mouth got ahead of my manners. "I thought a crazy old guy with a bunch of cats lived here," I blurted out.

Mack laughed. "I'm crazy and I'm old, and my wife and I used to have many, many cats. I still have five. They're probably hiding from Archie and Elvis. My cats and I live on the first floor. My wife was terribly allergic to dogs, so we made this floor Scooter's floor. It is also Ben's floor and my son-in-law, Thomas's, floor. Ben's mother, my daughter, died three years ago. We wanted to do anything we could to keep Benito close to us. That's why we remodeled this floor to be their living quarters."

I was in awe that Ben had a place like this to live in, but when I learned that his mother was dead, I didn't feel like he was so lucky.

"And Ben's grandmother?" I asked.

"My wife, Brenda. She died of breast cancer last summer."

"I am truly sorry," I said.

"Benito's been through so much in his life. I don't want him to have to worry about Scooter," Mack said, thumping his fist on the table. It hit so hard it startled the dogs—and me.

"If you give me the information, I can go home and make a flyer right away. I already drew a couple of pictures of Scooter," I said. Ben had let me do a couple of sketches for my school art project. I had promised he could have the best one when my project was done.

"I don't think a flyer will be necessary this time," Mack said.

"Why? Has something already happened to Scooter?"

"No, no. I don't think anything is going to happen to him, although I'm sure he'd rather be home," Mack said. "The dognapper has already called and made a ransom demand."

"Oh, no. For how much?"

"The amount isn't important. I have enough, as you might imagine. But he, or she, won't return Scooter until tomorrow," Mack said.

"He or she? But if the dognapper called, couldn't you tell if it was a man or a woman?" I asked.

"It doesn't seem important," Mack said.

"You have to tell Ben!" Now I was mad. "I believe you let him go searching for Scooter when know Scooter will be returned tomorrow."

"I told you, I don't want Ben to worry. It's bette he thinks Scooter is lost. This way, I can get the mon to the thief first, and make sure I can get Scooter ba safely. When the time is right, and I'm sure that I've p an end to all of this, I will tell Benito," Mack said.

"All of this?" I asked. "Do you think the dognapper is the same person who took Boris and Daphne?"

I hesitated a moment, then asked the question I really wanted to ask. "Wasn't there a ransom demand for Daphne as well?"

Mack looked surprised. "A ransom for Daphne?" he asked. "What makes you say that? Jennifer offered a generous reward, and that helped bring Daphne home."

"When I saw you the other night, it looked like Jennifer was giving you ransom money."

Mack laughed, a warm full laugh. "Oh, my dear girl. I wasn't getting a ransom. I was *giving* Jennifer money so that she could match Ted's reward. She felt it was the only way that she would get Daphne back. And it seems she may have been right."

Mack sighed, and then went on. "I have no idea who

Usually on TV, the person who arrives with the ransom money is jittery, looking around nervously, and drawing all kinds of attention to himself. Not Mack. He calmly stood about six feet from the Lenin statue.

"Now!" someone called. Apparently it was the command Mack had expected. He took an envelope out of his coat pocket and held it up in his left hand. He kept it up there.

A knight on a unicycle pedaled soundlessly across the square, snatched the envelope, and continued around the corner.

I am not making this up. You can't make this kind of stuff up. I'd just seen Ben's grandfather make a handoff to a cycling knight while Lenin looked on.

As ridiculous as it seemed, the knight costume was the perfect disguise. People were always wearing wacky things in Fremont, so nobody would really take notice. And with the helmet covering most of the person's face, it was impossible to identify the individual. I couldn't even tell if it was a man or a woman.

I watched as Mack dialed a number on the cell phone. I hoped it was to tell Ben to come home. Scooter would be back tomorrow.

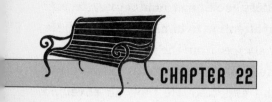

CHAPTER 22

ELVIS, WHO HAD BEEN UNUSUALLY QUIET ON FRIDAY (DESPITE THE KNIGHT on a unicycle), was back to barking and howling the next morning in the backseat of our Honda. I was going in to the animal shelter early because we didn't have either a game or practice that weekend.

We pulled into the parking lot at the Elliott Bay Animal Shelter. The sheer excitement of being around so many dogs and cats must have inspired Elvis to howl. Or maybe it was the shiny silver Lexus convertible that pulled in next to us.

"Elvis, quiet!" Mom commanded him in a gentle voice. Amazingly, it worked. Until the driver got out of the Lexus. The dog went bonkers again when he saw it was Meredith. Meredith driving a new convertible? Either pet grooming paid better than I realized or my suspicions about Meredith were on target.

"Great car!" I said, hopping out of the Honda. It must

be brand-new from the dealer, since it still had Seattle Lexus plates on it, and a license number on paper taped to the back window. "Do you mind if I let Elvis out to say hello?"

"I'd love to see Elvis!" Meredith said. She seemed in an extra-good mood.

We walked into the shelter together. "Are you feeling better today?" I asked.

"What?"

"I stopped by the shop yesterday with Archie and Elvis. Arlene said you were out sick," I said.

"I'm much, much better today. In fact, I feel great. It was just a twenty-four-hour thing."

"Meredith!" the receptionist gushed when we walked in. "I'm so happy you could come in today. The director is making a special trip down here to thank you personally."

"It's nothing," Meredith said, practically beaming.

"Hannah, I have some good news," Leonard said. I followed him back to a small office. He handed me an envelope. A snapshot fell out of the inside card when I opened it. A photo of Izzie with an adorable little girl hugging her.

"Izzie's new family loved the sketch you did of her. I told them about the great volunteer we had here who had such a strong connection to Izzie. They said they'd love to meet you and your mom," Leonard said. "If it's okay with your mom, I'd like to give your phone number to Izzie's new owners. They may want to invite you over or something."

"Thank you! That's great," I said.

I was on a roller coaster of emotions today. I woke up worried about Scooter, then I worried about Izzie, and now I was happy about Izzie. I went back to worrying about Scooter.

"We have a new arrival this morning. Meredith found him and brought him in earlier. He's in great shape, and he's probably just lost, not abandoned, judging by how he looks and behaves. You can start today by spending some time with him," Leonard said. I followed him down to the kennels where the dogs are kept. "Here's the big guy."

"Scooter!" I was thrilled to see him, but totally surprised to see him at the shelter.

Scooter, on the other hand, just seemed thrilled. The shaggy dog leaped to attention, jumped so that his front legs were on my shoulders, and started licking my face.

CHAPTER 23

"HOW DID SCOOTER GET HERE?"

"You know this dog?" Leonard asked.

"You bet I know him. I know his owners, too," I said.

"That's great, because he didn't have a collar or any identification tag or a pet license on him," he said. "So, tell me who to call."

I pulled out my cell phone and scrolled through the recently dialed calls to find Mack's cell phone number. I gave the number to Leonard, but there was no answer.

"I know! I can call my mom. She can go to their house and tell them that Scooter's here. Or maybe I can just have my mom come and pick him up."

"As much as I trust you and your mom, I'm not authorized to release this dog to anyone other than his owners," Leonard said. "Go ahead and call your mom, though, and see if she can contact Scooter's owners."

After all that had happened in the past three weeks, I appreciated how careful the shelter was about things like this.

I got my mom on the phone just as she was pulling into the parking garage under PCC and our apartment. "I'll run up to the house right now," she said. "Wait. I still have the phone number Ben gave me yesterday when you asked to go to his grandfather's house. You can call that number, but I'll still run up there so we make sure we get the good news to them."

I dialed the number for Ben's house, and Ben's dad answered.

"Yes!" his dad screamed into the phone when I told him where Scooter was. "Ben and I will be there as fast as we can. Probably in fifteen or twenty minutes." He hadn't completely hung up the phone when I heard his dad calling, "Ben! Scooter's back! We can go get him now!"

Leonard gave me permission to have Scooter hang out with me since he was only going to be there for fifteen more minutes. My volunteer assignment for the morning was to help get invitations ready for a fund-raising party. I'd rather do something to directly help an animal, but when you're a volunteer you end up doing all kinds of things to help the organization. I went to the supply closet, Scooter by my side, to get more envelopes.

"Meredith, look who's here! Remember Scooter?" I asked. I watched Meredith's face closely, trying to gauge her reaction to my seemingly innocent comment.

Scooter, the most mild-mannered dog in the world, actually growled.

"He must be a little skittish of me since his last grooming," Meredith said, laughing awkwardly. "He probably thinks I'm about to give him a bath or something."

"Here she is!" said a woman as she came through the front door. "Meredith, I've heard so much about you as a volunteer, and on top of everything you've done you're making such a magnanimous donation to us! Imagine, another eighty-five hundred dollars for our shelter! It's absolutely wonderful."

Had she said $8,500? I started adding something in my head, but Meredith's voice interrupted my calculations.

"The amount has increased," Meredith said quietly. Everyone waited expectantly. The envelope stuffers in the workroom probably needed more envelopes, but I waited, too. "It's now closer to thirteen thousand. It's twelve thousand seven hundred fifty dollars." The handful of people in the room broke into spontaneous applause. Scooter started barking, something I'd never heard him do before. He ran to the front door, where he could see Ben and his father.

"Thank you for all your kind words," Meredith was saying. "But it's really all my pleasure. If you'll excuse me now, I have some dogs to bathe." Everyone laughed.

Just as Meredith left the front area, Ben walked in. I can't imagine a dog or a guy being any happier than they were. Leonard came out with some paperwork for Ben's dad to sign.

"I don't know much about where Scooter was found, Mr. Campo," Leonard said. "Let me find our volunteer who brought him in, and she can give us the rest of the story."

A car in the parking lot kicked up gravel as it pulled away.

"I think she just left," I said.

"We can get details later. All that matters is that we have him back. Thank you so much for keeping him safe until we could get here," Ben's dad said, pumping Leonard's arm.

Leonard patted Scooter on the rump. "Stay out of trouble, big guy."

"I'm so happy he's back," Ben said. "But what happened to him is still a mystery."

"I think this mystery is about to end," I said. Then I went back to work.

CHAPTER 24

IF I THOUGHT $8,500 WAS AN INTERESTING NUMBER, I FOUND THE FIGURE $12,750 extra intriguing. I jotted down some numbers after I finished putting five hundred invitations into five hundred envelopes.

Reward money for Boris: $4,250

Jennifer had had to match what Ted offered in order to get Daphne back safely.

Reward money for Daphne: $4,250

That brings us to the $8,500 mark. If Mack had to pay the same price for Scooter, that would bring the total to $12,750. The same amount Meredith had just donated to the Elliott Bay Animal Shelter.

A coincidence? I think not.

After lunch, Leonard assigned me to help Meredith with bathing the dogs. "She's back now," he said. I think he was giving me an extra reward with that assignment. What a fun job. And what perfect timing.

I waited until we had a seventy-five-pound black dog named Newton in the washtub to bring anything up.

"Nice car you had this morning. Is it new?" I asked.

"Brand-new. I ran into some extra money," she said.

Curiouser and curiouser.

"That was an interesting amount of money you donated today," I said, in what I hoped was a friendly, conversational mode.

"Just happened to be what I had available," she said.

Uh-huh.

I decided to go for it, TV-detective style.

"Meredith, how did you figure out it was Mack who fronted the reward money for Daphne?" I asked, abruptly changing the subject. It was a technique to catch her off guard.

She dropped the nozzle. Water sprayed out toward me. Maybe this wasn't the best time to get the facts.

"What are you talking about? Do you mean Mack, the old guy who hangs out at Costas Opa?"

I sighed. "You can be straight with me. I know you collected the reward money for the missing dogs. The rewards for Boris and Daphne equal the amount the shelter thought you were donating. But once you demanded that Mack match the reward price of the other two dogs, you upped it to that interesting figure of twelve thousand seven hundred fifty dollars. Not twelve thousand, or even twelve thousand five hundred. But twelve thousand seven hundred fifty. Exactly three times the amount of the original reward money, equal to the reward money for three dogs."

If only Lily could see me now. I was in acting mode, playing the part of a confident detective who has all the loose ends tied up. Truth is, I was still guessing on most of it. It'd be pretty embarrassing if I was wrong.

I didn't think I was wrong, though. Meredith's face was flushed red, and her jaw was set tight. I continued: "I don't know why or how you kidnapped those dogs. But I know that you were the one who got the money for them. And I think you're scrubbing this dog too hard."

She eased up a bit on the scrubbing. I didn't ease up.

"Once you made easy money with Boris, you just kept going. I just don't know how you figured out that Mack had something to do with Jennifer's reward."

She didn't say anything.

"I don't even know who to call to turn you in," I said. "Most of all, I don't know why you would do such a thing. If you love animals so much, why would you rip them from their safe homes and loving families?"

She helped Newton out of the tub. I handed her a couple of towels, and she started drying him. "People don't deserve the animals they have," she muttered. "I would never hurt an animal. I borrowed those little dogs only to make a point. The reward money for Boris was a nice surprise."

"You might have treated the dogs kindly, but their owners were out of their minds with worry about them," I said. "Ted, Jennifer, and Ben love their dogs deeply. They take good care of them."

She didn't say anything. I had one last thing to say.

"Meredith, I've made up my mind. I'm not going to turn you in," I said. She looked relieved. "You're going to turn yourself in."

I know I have no power to make Meredith do anything. I'm not even very threatening. Still, I was pretty sure she was going to do the right thing.

"What makes you think she'll admit it all?" Mom asked as we drove home late that afternoon.

"Mack's going to help me with that," I said. "You'll see."

CHAPTER 25

BEN'S FAMILY INVITED MY FAMILY TO DINNER THAT NIGHT.

"My grandpa is going to order a bunch of Indian food from Tandoor," he said when he called. "Dad says to bring Elvis, too. We've got some raw bones to keep the dogs occupied and out of trouble."

At seven o'clock, Mom, Elvis, Lily (she seems like family), and I entered the gate to the Mack Pappas, Thomas Campo, and Benito Campo yard. I wasn't sure if we were supposed to go around to the back and upstairs to where Ben and his dad lived, or ring the front door-bell. As if in answer to my unasked question, the front door swung open and Scooter came bounding out. Mack stood at the doorway. "Welcome, welcome! Come in. The food just arrived, and we're just setting up."

The first floor of the house was even more magnificent than upstairs. I didn't get much time to ogle because Mack ushered us back toward the kitchen. You could tell that this part of the house is where people actually lived. The kitchen opened to a comfy area for reading, watching television, and hanging out.

We helped set up a buffet with the takeout containers of Indian food. I piled my plate with vegetable *pakora*, eggplant *bharta*, and the most delicious spinach *nan* (yummy flatbread) I've ever tasted. We squeezed around the dining-room table, with Elvis and Scooter just feet away gnawing on their bones.

"Is it all set up now?" I asked Mack.

"Yes. As soon as we have the word that Meredith has contacted the police on her own, I'll make a donation of twenty-five thousand dollars to the Elliott Bay Animal Shelter," Mack said.

"So that's how you did it," Mom said quietly, squeezing my hand. I could tell by the tone of her voice that she was pleased with my plan and how it was shaping up.

"Wasn't the money Meredith was donating yours to start with?" Lily asked Mack.

"Just the money for Daphne and Scooter. Ted used his savings to be sure he'd get Boris back. But it doesn't matter where the money came from: it wasn't Meredith's to give away."

"How did she figure out you were the benefactor behind Jennifer's reward?" Lily asked.

"I don't know. Maybe she figured it out the same way Hannah did," Mack said.

Everyone looked at me. I tipped an imaginary hat on my head.

"How about that car she was driving this morning? Has she been doing this for a while and banking most of the money for herself?" Mom asked.

"I think I can answer that one," Ben's dad said. It turned out that Tom Campo was a private investigator. He had done some digging around and had found that Meredith had a $4 million trust fund.

"Wow," Lily said.

"I know. It's a lot of money," Tom agreed.

"No, not that. I meant 'wow' that you're a private eye," she said.

"Seems like I'm not the only detective around here," he said, winking at me. "I may, however, be the only licensed private detective at the table tonight."

One of Tom's friends at the police station was going to let him know when Meredith had held up her end of the bargain and admitted what she had done. As soon as that happened, Mack was going to write the check for the donation. Meredith had already returned Ted's money to him.

"I've already drafted the letter to go with it," Mack

said, holding up a business letter. "It outlines how this money is donated in loving memory of Elizabeth Pappas Campo and Brenda MacMillan Pappas."

"Thanks, Mack," Tom said. He seemed a little choked up.

Ben got up and went around the table to give Mack a big hug. "Thank you, Grandpa. Thank you for making sure that Scooter—and all of the other dogs around here—will be safe."

CHAPTER 26

OUR FOURTH WEEK IN FREMONT WAS MUCH MORE RELAXED. SO WAS THE second month. My dog-walking business had picked up again, but I didn't take on as many canine clients as I had earlier. I decided I needed more time to draw and read and play Frisbee.

A few Saturdays later, Mom picked me up at three o'clock after my volunteer job at the animal shelter. "I have a surprise for you," she said. I looked in the backseat, but all I saw was Elvis and an empty water bottle.

"Tell me. Please."

"We're going to see Izzie," Mom said.

"Izzie the dog? Now? Really? How?" I was so excited!

"I got a call from Libby and Calvin, the couple who adopted Izzie. Leonard had already told them about you, and they wanted to make sure you didn't lose contact with her. They invited us to come over today because it's such a nice day. They thought Elvis and Izzie could meet each other and play outside," Mom said.

"I bet Elvis will love romping around without a leash on, won't you?" I scratched him behind his ears.

We drove across town to Capitol Hill. Mom parked just down the street from a park in front of a huge brick house.

Izzie sat on the front steps, looking at me for a few seconds. Then she lunged toward me. I hugged her like I never wanted to let her go.

"Do you know my dog?" a little girl asked.

"Is Izzie your dog?"

"Yes, Izzie is." She giggled and kept repeating "Izzie is, Izzie is."

"I'm Libby." A woman crossed the yard toward us. "You must be Hannah and Maggie. You've already met Rachel. And of course you know Izzie."

I was in heaven. Elvis was pretty happy, too. Libby invited us to the backyard, which was fenced in, so Elvis could, indeed, run free. I played with the dogs and with Rachel, who turned out to be darn cute and funny for a four-year-old. I'd tuned out the grown-ups' conversation, until I heard Libby say, "Maggie, I didn't know you were house-sitters. How very interesting. I have someone I'd love you to meet." Libby asked if I'd watch Rachel while she took Mom next door to meet the neighbors.

Later, as we settled into the car, I asked, "What was all that about? You know, going next-door and all?"

"Their next door neighbors are going to Switzerland for a couple of months. Some kind of business trip. It just might be a house-sitting opportunity for us," Mom said. "We'll see."

"Could anything be more perfect?" I asked. "You and me living next door to Izzie. Living in the big house. It's just too perfect."

Elvis moaned a little. "Of course, living with Elvis in Fremont is going to be hard to top," I said.

Elvis put his drool-covered chin on my shoulder, and we headed back to our temporary home, the Center of the Universe.